FACES

Diane Winger

Books by
Charlie and Diane Winger

Fiction

Rockfall
   (by Diane Winger)

Non-Fiction (Memoir)

Two Shadows – the inspirational story of one man's triumph over adversity
   (by Charlie Winger)

Guidebooks / Adventure Photography

Highpoint Adventures – The Complete Guide to the 50 State Highpoints

The Essential Guide to Great Sand Dunes National Park & Preserve

The Trad Guide to Joshua Tree – 60 Favorite Climbs from 5.5 to 5.9

Because It's There - A Photographic Journey

Visit **The Winger Bookstore** on the web at:
WingerBookstore.com

To Charlie,
for always reminding me
that life is an adventure.
I love you, man.

In Memory of Gretchen —
I think of you
whenever I see a wildflower.

CHAPTER 1

"Matt, you're on belay."

Jessica listened for his response. "Climbing!" he called.

"Climb on."

She couldn't stop smiling as she took in rope through the belay device she had rigged to an anchor system at the top of the climb. *We're in Joshua Tree!* Jessica had managed to schedule two full weeks of vacation from work during prime rock climbing time in her favorite location. Six Colorado climbing friends had converged on this southern California climbers' Mecca, miraculously snagged two adjacent campsites in the coveted Hidden Valley Campground, and were wrapping up their first full day of climbing on a route named *Double Cross*.

"Jam your fist into that crack. It'll hold!" she advised the struggling climber below.

Matt was an excellent climber in the indoor gyms, but had just started venturing outdoors in the past few weeks. He had scoffed at the relatively easy rating of *Double Cross* when Jessica and Allison led the way to its base, but now he was discovering the challenges of crack climbing. Jessie remembered her early years learning the techniques of this unique aspect of the sport. A more experienced climber told her, "Most climbing comes pretty naturally — like going up stairs or a ladder. But climbing a narrow, vertical crack is different from anything you've done before. The only way to learn to climb cracks is by climbing lots of cracks." And she had.

"Falling!" he screamed.

Jessica chuckled. "I've got you — you're not going anywhere!" Matt's hands had slipped out of the crack, and he had fallen about a foot lower simply because the rope securing him had stretched a bit. "Form your right hand into a wedge-shape, like we practiced. If that feels too loose in the crack, rotate your hand and form a fist instead."

Matt inched his way higher. Finally, after a few more "falls" — which he managed without the screaming — he pulled himself onto the large ledge where Jessica was secured to the anchor. He was huffing like a steam engine.

"Move around behind me and clip in to the chains. I'll belay Allison while you catch your breath."

Jessica retrieved the second rope which Matt had trailed behind him, and efficiently rearranged the belay system to bring Allison up the climb. Once she heard Matt's breathing return to something resembling normal, she untied from the first rope and asked him to use it to set up a rappel.

Allison made steady progress, and didn't need the coaching that Matt had required. Jessica took the opportunity to look around as she manipulated the belay rope. She loved the view from this high perch above the desert valley. The gangly-shaped Joshua Trees below created an other-worldly scene, beautiful and strange. Towering, pale rock formations were scattered all around, their dramatic shapes, cracks, twists, and bulges offering thousands of possibilities for climbing. Bands of tiny, yellow flowers offered splashes of color along the valley floor.

Brilliant orange-red blooms on a patch of claret cup cactus growing along a sandy wash glowed like small fires, visible even from her high perch. Jessica had been coming to Joshua Tree National Park for almost ten years, and never grew tired of the scenery.

As Allison topped out, Jessica inquired, "Did either of you bring up any water? I'm parched."

"Nope, sorry," they both concurred.

"Rope!" Matt called out the usual warning to anyone below as he tossed the coiled ends of the rappel rope out from the wall. He had threaded the rope through two steel rings attached to the rock by heavy chains and bolts. With the midpoint of the rope being looped through the anchor at the top of the climb, they could now set up a system to slide down the two equal halves of the rope using friction devices to easily control their descent.

"Jessie, why don't you rap down first," Allison offered. "You led the climb and acted as our belay slave all this time. Go for it."

"Um, the rope is caught on that ledge near the bottom of the climb," Matt noted. "Should I try throwing it again?"

Jessica peered over the edge, studying the jumble of rope far below. "No, that'll be okay. I can untangle it when I get down to that point. Did you knot the ends of the rope?"

"Oh. I forgot."

"Never mind. I know my rope is long enough — look at how much is piled up down there. And it's only about ten or fifteen feet from the ledge to the ground. No problem."

She rearranged her gear, forced the two sides of the rappel rope through her friction device and clipped it to her harness. She double-checked everything before unclipping her specialized sling known as a personal safety device (or P.A.S.) from the anchor, and started down.

"See you back at camp!" a voice shouted from below.

Jessica glanced over her shoulder as she continued her descent. Marilyn, her closest friend and long-time climbing partner, was sauntering along a path in the valley, moving with her characteristically cat-like grace. Even without hearing her familiar, gravelly voice, Jessie could spot Marilyn a mile away by her walk, her stance, and especially her expressive hand gestures. She and the other two climbers in their Colorado contingent were returning from a visit to *The Bong*, where Marilyn had been coaching Paul on his first "lead" crack climb. As usual, Marilyn was stopping to point out plants along their way. Ever the botanist.

Jessica waved her free left hand in reply, then focused on the tangle of rope by her feet. She tightened her grasp on the pair of ropes in her right "brake" hand held low beside her hip, and began picking at the jumble. She manipulated herself further to the left. *I need to be a little lower*, she thought, and let the ropes slide through her right hand a bit further.

Suddenly, she felt a rope end rush through her grasp. Her brake hand tightened in panic around a single strand of rope as her body began to topple. She clawed desperately at the parallel ropes she could still see above her, but the two became one in an instant. She glimpsed the intense blue of the California sky for a moment before an extreme blow to her back forced her lungs to expel all their air.

The next thing she was aware of was Marilyn's face hovering over her. Someone else was there, too, with hands gripped on both sides of her helmet, holding her head securely in position.

"Jessie, talk to me. Can you hear me? Jessie!"

Her eyes darted around. Someone hovered over her, staring into her face. "Jessie, talk to me."

Jessica groaned. The face above her began to come into focus.

"Jess, where do you hurt?"

Jessica took a moment to respond. "My back ... head hurts." She moaned and closed her eyes. The bright light made her head feel even worse.

"Okay. We've called Search and Rescue, and they're on the way. Jessie, do you know who I am? Look at me."

She squinted. "Marilyn. My best friend." She looked around again and tried to roll onto her side. "Hey, let go of my head!"

"No, no, no. Lie still. Paul's going to keep your head and neck stable until we hear otherwise from the EMTs. Relax. Deep breaths. You're going to be okay. Now, can you wiggle your toes for me? Good! Now your fingers. Excellent."

"Head hurts," she mumbled.

She focused on the rock face towering above her, her eyes following the crack named *Double Cross* as it rose up and up. Two shorter, parallel, horizontal cracks sliced across it, like a Russian Orthodox cross. *I guess I've just been double crossed,* she thought as she closed her eyes again.

***

The funny thing, Jessica said to herself as she lay in a hospital room the next morning, is that I really don't remember anything after they loaded me on the back board until the doctors were running all those tests in the ER.

"Hello, Ms. Stein. I'm Dr. Goldman. Do you remember when we talked last night?"

She remembered a parade of doctors and nurses stopping to check her out last night — too many to keep straight. She thought Dr. Goldman could have been the one who came by just before they turned the lights down. "Yes. Can I go home?" Jessica replied, trying to ignore the throbbing of her head and queasy stomach she felt whenever she spoke. This was worse than any hangover she'd ever had.

"I need to take a look at your eyes again and ask you some more questions. And if we release you, you must promise me that you'll fly back to Denver as soon as you can get a flight out and call your primary physician to follow up. You were extremely lucky that you didn't break any bones or have any internal injuries, but we are concerned about the concussion, and you need to follow up on that if you have any of the symptoms we discussed."

"I know. I'll head home. I'll call my doctor. I promise."

Dr. Goldman shone his penlight in her eyes, had her follow the light's movements, and used both hands to gently feel the back of her skull and her neck. "Okay, I'm going to let you go home in a few hours. Someone will be coming in with your release papers, and to go over the instructions again with you. We'll keep you on the IV for a little longer, since you were so dehydrated when you came in. Do you have any questions?"

"No, Doctor. Thanks for everything."

CHAPTER 2

"You can go in now," Dr. Goldman said, as he walked out of Jessica's hospital room. Marilyn virtually leaped into the room, her energy level cranked up a notch higher than usual, if that was even possible.

"Hey — I hear you're busting out of this place! Not that I was eavesdropping out in the hallway or anything."

"Yep. You can't keep ... a good woman down." She cupped both hands over her temples and closed her eyes. "I need to rebook my flight home. Can you help?"

Marilyn pulled out her smart phone and exhibited some flashy finger work over its screen. "I was just waiting for the word." More prestidigitation ensued. "All right. We're confirmed on a flight this evening. Done deal!"

Jessica opened her eyes again. "Wait a minute — 'we'? Mar, you don't need to cut your vacation short. I'll be fine by myself. Someone can pick me up at the airport and..."

"No way, Jess-say. You're my main climbing partner, my best friend, my *Sista*. I'm not leaving your side until I've heard from your doc that your brain is back to its happy self again."

Jessica sighed, but grinned. "Okay, but I owe you — big time!"

They heard a bit of a commotion in the hallway, and in popped the other four members of their Colorado climbing party.

"We have a present for you, Jessie," they declared, almost in unison. Allison handed over Jessica's climbing helmet with a ribbon attached and a colorful envelope tied to the other end.

Jessica opened and read the get-well card, pondering the notes each of her friends had written inside. She unfolded a piece of paper that had been tucked in the envelope with the card. "Good for one new climbing helmet. New skull not included," it read.

"Obviously, you'll be retiring your current 'brain bucket.' Check out the crack."

She grimaced slightly at the slang term that she had often used herself. Jessica ran a finger along the crack on the back of her helmet, considering what might have happened if she had not been wearing it when she fell. The EMTs and medical staff had painted an extremely sobering picture for her, extolling the virtues of this vital piece of equipment. Yes, she'd definitely need a new helmet, but this one would be kept as a precious memento.

Her friends queried about her health, told their versions of what had happened, and offered up a few stories from the previous night's dinnertime at camp sans Marilyn, who had — Jessica now learned — spent the night in a visitor area of the hospital. When it became apparent that Jessica was getting fatigued, they offered their good wishes, hugged her gently, and retreated to head back up into the Park for another climbing day.

"I'll let you get some rest, and see you in a little bit," Marilyn said.

"Wait. I need to tell you something." Jessica had a worried frown on her face.

Marilyn pulled a chair close to the bed. "What's going on?"

"Everyone who was just here... They — I mean, I..."

"It's okay, Jess. Just spit it out."

"Who *were* those people?"

Marilyn stared at her, frowning in concern.

"Seriously, Jess? That was Allison, Matt, Paul, and Brian."

Jessica frowned in puzzlement. "Really?"

"You didn't recognize them?"

"I don't remember seeing *any* of them before — ever!" Now Jessica looked closer to panic than simply worry.

"Do you recognize *me*?" Marilyn asked, puzzled.

Jessica relaxed a bit as she stared at her friend. "Yeah. You're Marilyn Monroe. How could I forget that beauty mark, cascading blonde hair, and voluptuous figure?"

Marilyn laughed in relief at the familiar, good-natured ribbing. She had long ago shared the story of her first name with Jessica, and it had been a source of amusement ever since. When her father got his first look at his newborn daughter, he immediately noticed her tiny facial mole, positioned just like the famous beauty mark of the glamorous icon. Combined with her miniscule wisps of white-blonde hair atop her head, he declared that she was surely another Marilyn Monroe. The truth was that this Marilyn — Marilyn Morrison — had grown into a tall, lean, athletic "jock" with a shape that could sometimes be mistaken for a young man's. Her blonde hair had darkened a bit as she grew up, and she wore it in a casual, short style. No cascades.

"Didn't they tell you that you might have some memory issues for a week or two after the concussion? I'm sure that was just a temporary thing. Don't let it worry you."

"Yeah, you're right. By the time this fun-filled vacation is over, and I get back to work, this will all be nothing but a bad 'memory'."

Marilyn groaned at the pun. "Okay, now get some rest and I'll go see what kind of mess the gang left in our rental car. They packed up our camping gear this morning for us and brought it down from the Park. I'll see you in a bit."

"Thanks for everything, Mar. You're a great friend — I don't care what everyone else says about you."

"See, I knew you'd be back to your old self soon. Later, Sista."

CHAPTER 3

During the three hour drive back to Las Vegas and the hours spent at the airport and on the flight home to Denver, the two friends had plenty of time to discuss the questions which were on both their minds — how did Jessie's accident happen? What did she remember? What had Marilyn witnessed from her vantage point?

As for the first question, both agreed that the rappel rope must have been set up unevenly, with one end hanging far longer than the other.

"I should have checked the set-up and looked for the middle-mark on the rope. And I don't know why I didn't insist on pulling the rope back up so we could tie knots in the ends. I know better." Jessica leaned back in her seat, closing her eyes and massaging her temples gently.

Marilyn came to her defense. "Well, as you said, you thought you were seeing plenty of rope on that ledge, and didn't think there could be any problem reaching the ground."

"The short end must have been hidden in the tangle. Dumb, dumb, dumb. I should have seen that something was wrong," Jessica continued, becoming more agitated.

"Yeah, and Matt should have set up the system right in the first place!"

Jessica took several deep breaths, and turned to look at her friend. "I hope everyone isn't blaming him for this. How's he doing? Was he the one who hung back by the doorway when everyone came to see me in the hospital?" Marilyn nodded. "I need to give him a call when he gets back to Denver, and let him know I don't blame him for what happened."

Jessica dozed off and on during the hours of travel. When she'd awaken, she'd ask Marilyn for more details. Had she remained conscious? Yes, but she hadn't responded to questions for the first few minutes, other than to look around as if she were seeing the people and rock formations around her for the first time. Marilyn, in turn, asked if she remembered when they were carefully unclipping climbing gear from her harness, and asking her to wiggle her toes and fingers. No, but she remembered when the EMTs arrived and strapped her on the back-board, then the dizzying ride as they carried her over and around boulders to the waiting ambulance. But things were a bit vague after that, until she found herself in the ER and a bevy of medical personnel had inserted IVs, run scans, poked, prodded, and asked questions about everything from the current date to her entire life's medical history.

It was after 10 p.m. when they finally arrived at Jessica's house in southeast Denver. Marilyn pulled her Subaru into the driveway. "Let's just leave our gear in the car till morning. I'll get our clothing bags."

Jessica rose stiffly from the passenger seat and headed to her front door, fumbling in the dark with her house key. "Pooka — I'm home!" The gray tabby dashed into the living room to greet her, remembered that he needed to teach 'Mom' a lesson for leaving on a trip, and retreated to his food dish. "Didn't Della pay enough attention to you while I was gone?" she called. She'd have to remember to call her neighbor in the morning to let her know that she didn't need to keep checking on Pooka for the next two weeks after all.

Marilyn had insisted on spending the night, using the excuse that she was too tired to drive the additional ten minutes back to her own house. Both knew that she just wanted to keep an eye on Jessie, and make sure she was doing all right. Although the doctor had said that it wasn't necessary to wake Jessica throughout the night, he had emphasized that it would be a major concern if it was difficult to awaken her in the morning. Marilyn wanted to be there when morning arrived.

Jessica awakened to the smell of fresh coffee and bright sunlight streaming into her room. Pooka was perched by her pillow, staring intently into her face, purring at full volume. Apparently, she had been forgiven for going on a trip. Marilyn had come into her room and watched her sleeping for a minute before drawing open the curtains. "That coffee smells wonderful!"

"Well, I know how much you love the smell of coffee. Maybe someday you'll actually decide you like how it tastes, too." She grinned as she brought her personalized mug over to the bed so Jessica could truly savor the aroma. Jessie kept a coffee maker and all the usual fixings in her house so that friends who were addicted to their morning brews wouldn't have to suffer. The mug in Marilyn's hands was also a permanent resident.

The rest of the morning was filled with phone calls to her neighbor, Della (thanking her for looking in on the cat) and to Jessica's family physician's office (setting a quickly-arranged appointment for that afternoon). Marilyn unloaded and unpacked much of Jessica's gear and clothing, dropped off her own items at her house, then returned with a load of groceries, ready to shuttle her to the doctor's office later. Jessica was under orders not to drive until her own doctor gave her the all-clear.

It was an unseasonably warm day, and they took advantage of it by eating a late lunch on the back porch, where they admired a few early spring crocuses which had poked up in the garden just in the few days they had been gone to California.

As they came back into the house, the doorbell rang. "I've got it," Jessica offered, since her friend's hands were full, carrying a tray of dirty plates and dishes to the kitchen.

She squinted through the peephole in her front door. A gray-haired woman with glasses was standing on the porch, holding something in front of her. She didn't look familiar, but seemed harmless, so Jessica opened the door.

"Jessica! You were so vague about why you were back so early from your trip that I got worried. Is everything all right?" she exclaimed in a deep, contralto voice.

Jessie knew that voice well. But she was flustered that she hadn't recognized her next-door neighbor, Della Giambrocco, before hearing her speak. "Come on in. Everything's fine."

Della was carrying a covered plate, undoubtedly filled with some sort of scrumptious baked goodies. Jessica figured her neighbor seldom let a day go by without baking something wonderful. She usually ended up taking many of the treats to work to share — otherwise she'd weigh about 400 pounds by now.

The older woman headed to the kitchen table where she uncovered the plate. A small bundle wrapped in aluminum foil was tucked by the edge of the pastries. As soon as she began opening it up, a gray streak of cat rushed into the kitchen and Pooka began an enthusiastic do-si-do dance around the women's ankles, complete with his own musical accompaniment.

"Pooka, *amore mio*. Yes, Della brought you a treat, too," she cooed, as she delivered the packet of what appeared to be finely cut up brisket to the cat's dish.

"Della, you spoil him so much. No wonder he turns up his nose at kibble."

Her neighbor smiled broadly, then turned more serious. "Okay, but the main reason I stopped by is to find out why you came back so early."

"I just had a little accident, and thought it would be a good idea to take it easy instead of climbing. It's no big deal."

Marilyn interjected, "Sorry to be a party pooper, but we have that, um, *thing* we need to get to by two o'clock."

Jessica glanced at the kitchen clock. "Wow, I didn't realize what time it was. I'm sorry, Della. We're going to have to rush off. I'll come by tomorrow and visit with you for longer, if that's okay."

"Of course, dear. I'll talk to you soon," she said as she headed to the door.

"Thanks again for watching Pooka," Jessica called as her neighbor departed.

Then they were off to the doctor's office. A nurse entered the waiting room, called Jessica's name, and gave her a big smile as they walked back to an examination room. "How are you doing, Jessie? Have you been out climbing lately?"

Jessica managed a quick glance at the nurse's nametag. She was dismayed to read the all-too-familiar name there — Margaret. How could she not have recognized Margaret? She had been with Dr. Ehrlich for the entire decade or so that she had been going to him. They had often talked about her climbing, her work, and even the antics of her cat.

She recovered quickly, and launched into the usual conversation with the nurse, asking how her son was doing in college, and if her daughter still liked her job as a physical therapist. Then she briefly explained the reason for today's visit.

"I'll check to make sure they've sent us all of your test results. First, let's get your blood pressure, a pulse-oximeter reading, and a few other quick tests. Doctor will be in to talk with you in just a few minutes."

Jessica closed her eyes and breathed slowly and deeply after the nurse left the examination room. She tried to picture Dr. Ehrlich in her mind. Okay — white coat, stethoscope, slightly-receding hairline ... but she couldn't pull up any sort of visual memory of her family doctor's face.

A rap on the door was followed quickly by the entrance of a man in a white coat, stethoscope hung around his neck, with a slightly-receding hairline. Jessica was slightly relieved to realize that this man seemed *vaguely* familiar.

"Hello, Jessie. I understand you took a fall a few days ago. Tell me what happened." He sat on a padded stool, and rolled it over to where a laptop computer was set up.

"Well, I fell about ten feet or so from a ledge, and landed pretty much on my back. And, since my helmet ended up being cracked, I must have hit my head, too. Or at least hit the helmet."

"Did you remain conscious? I assume there were others there with you."

"Yes, several friends were close by. They tell me that my eyes were open, and I was kind of looking around, but wouldn't say anything for a few minutes. Then they started asking me questions like 'how many fingers am I holding up?' and 'where are you?'. I remember that part pretty clearly, and I think I passed their tests," she joked.

Dr. Ehrlich gazed at the computer screen, typed a few notes, clicked several times, and studied the reports and scan images which had been received from the hospital in the town of Joshua Tree, outside of the National Park. "Are you still having headaches?"

"Just a little. They've gotten a lot better, and I've switched to just taking some Tylenol a couple of times a day."

"Any other symptoms? Sensitivity to bright lights? Dizziness? Nausea?"

Jessica shook her head to each question. Those symptoms had faded away. He produced a pen light and repeated the tests she had undergone in the hospital as he asked more questions.

"Any problems with concentration? Have you gone back to work?

"Not yet. Actually, I'm on vacation for almost another two weeks."

"That's good. I'd like you to take it easy for the rest of your vacation time. You may find that you'll need to ease back into work. I can give you some information to provide to your employer, if you like. You're a computer programmer, aren't you?"

That was close enough of a description of her job. "Yes. But, I don't think I'll have a problem with work."

"All right, but keep that in mind, and don't push yourself too hard in the next several weeks, either mentally or physically. Are you sleeping okay? Feeling depressed or unusually angry? Is there anything you have questions or concerns about?"

She hesitated. *C'mon, Jess*, she said to herself. *Now is not the time to play tough. Tell him.*

"I'm sure this is just a bit of the confusion they told me I might experience for a little while after hitting my head," she started.

"What sort of confusion?" he prompted when she took a long pause.

"I'm having trouble recognizing people I should know."

"Can you give me some examples?"

"Well, I didn't recognize Margaret until she started talking to me about climbing and I read her nametag. And I didn't recognize you when you came in, either. Also, when several of my friends on the climbing trip came to see me in the hospital, I had no idea who they were."

"Let's take a look." Dr. Ehrlich studied the computer screen again. "Your vision tests they sent over look okay. Let's check again."

More familiar tests ensued. "There's nothing apparently wrong with your eyesight, but we can look into that further if we need to."

"I don't really think I'm having trouble with my vision. Everything seems to be in focus. I just can't seem to remember what people look like."

Dr. Ehrlich returned his attention to the computer, this time calling up what was clearly the results of a brain scan which Jessica remembered being done while she was in the ER. He turned back to her. "Jessica, I'm going to refer you to Dr. Nguyen. He's an excellent neurologist, and he'll be able to tell you a lot more than I can. Give this to the receptionist when you leave, and she'll get you set up with an appointment. Meanwhile, don't worry about this. It's not unusual to have some memory issues in the weeks following a concussion."

"Okay. I'll see what Dr. Nguyen has to say," she said, feeling frustrated at the likely delay in learning more about what was going on. "Oh — I almost forgot. The doctors in California told me not to drive until I got the okay from you."

"I assume you got a ride here today?" Jessica nodded. "I think it'll be fine, but let's give it until tomorrow to start driving again. And limit yourself to short trips — nothing more than fifteen or twenty minutes at a time for now."

"Okay, I'll take it easy. Thanks, Doc."

CHAPTER 4

Jessica rode home in silence. Marilyn had asked her how things went with the doctor when she returned to the waiting room, but quickly sensed her mood when she simply answered "okay" with a shrug, but didn't offer anything further. Marilyn didn't press her for more, knowing that her friend sometimes just needed to mull things over in silence when something was on her mind. It was a trait they shared, and both women cherished their ability to simply be with each other in silence when needed.

Marilyn dropped her off at home, with a final, "You need anything?" Jessica managed a thin smile and a brief, "No, I'm good. Thanks again for everything." They hugged, and Marilyn departed.

Jessica headed straight to the tiny bedroom she had set up as her home office, and booted up her laptop. She googled "trouble recognizing people." The first page of results was filled with articles about something called "prosopagnosia" or "face blindness." She was surprised to discover that an impairment in recognizing faces actually had a name. She skimmed several online articles, printing out a few, then created a new folder in her browser to store numerous other pages she bookmarked. When her headache returned and her eyes began to bother her, she glanced at her watch, surprised to realize that she had already been at the computer for almost an hour. Although her job as a software developer and designer often found her engrossed in her work in front of a computer screen for hours at a time, she realized that this fatigue was one of the expected symptoms of her recent concussion. Hopefully, this too would pass.

"C'mon, puss-puss," she whispered as she picked up the sleeping cat curled in her lap. "Let's both go take a nap."

***

Her appointment with Dr. Nguyen, the neurologist, was set for Friday of the following week. Jessica spent time each day perusing the articles she had bookmarked, finding that she could comfortably spend more time each day focusing on her self-assigned studies. After assurances from Jessica that she would be fine on her own, Marilyn had headed to Colorado's Western Slope to do some downhill and cross-country skiing with friends for what was left of her prematurely-aborted vacation time. Here in Denver, the weather was in full roller-coaster mode, offering up a warm day flirting with 70 degree temperatures, followed by a day of wet spring snow and wind. Today was somewhere in the middle, with yesterday's snow melting rapidly and noticeably greener grass peeking through the melted spots.

Jessica decided she needed some fresh air. She headed for an urban trail which passed close to her home. Gigantic cottonwood trees lined the path that ran for dozens of miles alongside a historic irrigation waterway — the Highline Canal. In a few more weeks, the old trees would produce a snowstorm of "cotton" that would pile up along the edge of the path like plowed snow. Today, the white patches beside the trail consisted of real snow.

She paused at a street crossing, waiting for several cars to pass before she hustled to pick up the trail again on the other side. She slowed her pace, then stopped as her head began to throb from the sudden exertion. She reversed course, and walked gently back to her house, taking care to avoid jarring movements.

After downing some Tylenol for her headache, Jessica lay down for a short time to let the pain subside. Before long, she returned to her research. She had discovered several do-it-yourself tests on the web related to prosopagnosia — face blindness — and worked through each one in her usual, competitive manner, determined to get as close to a "perfect" score as possible. Her passion for excellence had always been a trait that she credited for her outstanding grades in school. She was sorely disappointed with her performance on the face blindness tests.

The first test explored her ability to recognize the faces of famous people. It was self-scoring, since the emphasis wasn't on being able to remember their *names* accurately. The instructions explained that you could score an answer as "correct" if you saw, for example, Mick Jagger and remembered that he was the lead singer for the Rolling Stones, but couldn't bring his name to mind right away. You could also mark someone as "unfamiliar" if, even after being told their name, you didn't think you had seen their picture before.

Jessica found the celebrity test frustrating, and often surprising. Each photo was presented with an oval frame around the face, hiding features like big ears or distinctive hair styles. She managed to recognize Mahatma Gandhi (with his distinctive round glasses and nose that dominated his face) and Madonna (whose makeup, abundant blonde hair not quite hidden by the

21

oval frame, and gap between her front teeth were all traits she had noted in the past). That was it. Two out of thirty.

The second test was even more difficult for her. It presented computer-generated faces from different angles, and had her try to pick out faces she had already been shown. Even more faces were displayed for her to match. She suspected some had identical eyes as another, but other features were switched. Her score was again far below what was listed as "average." She realized that she could have achieved the same score purely by guessing, simply based on the mathematical odds for a multiple choice test.

The more she read, the more she believed that she had hit upon what was wrong with her. She was face blind.

***

Jessica glanced at the caller ID on her phone, her dismay almost convincing her to let the call go to voice mail. *I really should have called him.* "Hi Matt," she managed in an upbeat voice.

"Hey, Jessie. We're back from J-Tree and I wanted to check in to see how you're doing."

She kept her tone light. "I'm doing much better. The headaches are almost gone and the doc gave me the okay to drive. Yeah, doing great. How was the climbing?"

"We did a lot of top-roping after you two left, but nobody really wanted to lead anything." He cleared his throat. "Listen, Jessie. I just want to tell you how terrible I feel for what happened. I really thought I had enough length on both ends, but..."

"Hey, Matt. It's okay. Really!" she emphasized. "I missed it, too. We usually check each others' set up for tying in, rappels ...

everything. I guess we just got in a hurry. It's okay. We'll all be more careful in the future."

"Still, Jessie, I just want to apologize and let you know that I really hope you're going to be fine. I hope someday you'll be okay with climbing with me again. But I'll understand completely if you don't want to."

She heard the tightness in his voice. "Thanks, Matt. I don't have any problem at all with climbing with you again. Don't worry. We're still friends." Now she was starting to choke up a bit.

They both managed a few closing pleasantries and promised to talk again soon.

***

"These scans were run twelve days ago," Dr. Nguyen explained, "immediately after your accident. I'd like to see what this area of your brain looks like now. This will give me a better picture of your mTBI — Mild Traumatic Brain Injury — and how the healing has progressed."

The scan was followed by a series of cognitive tests administered by a very pleasant female technician. Or, perhaps there had actually been more than one female technician returning to the room as the tests progressed — Jessica no longer felt confident that she would notice as long as each technician wore the same medical garb as another.

Finally, the battery of tests was complete. She was escorted into Dr. Nguyen's office, where he sat at a desk, flipping through papers in a folder and peering at a now-familiar image on his computer screen — a brain. *Probably my sorry-ass brain,* Jessica thought.

"Jessica, your brain injury has improved considerably since your accident, and I'm pleased with the results of the cognitive tests you took today. I see no signs of problems with your visual or verbal skills, your motor skills are good, and your memory is fine."

Jessica let out a breath. She hadn't realized she hadn't been breathing while listening to the doctor's words.

"However," he began again. Jessica froze. "The facial recognition tests you took today and what I'm seeing in today's scan could indicate damage to an area of your brain called the fusiform gyrus." He turned the monitor so she could see it better. Jessica stared at the image. Her brain. Her ... *damaged* brain.

"Jessica, take a look at your CT scan. See this area near the lower rear of your brain?" He pointed with his pen. "This is the area that was affected by your concussion."

She knitted her brows and nodded slowly.

"This area is thought to be involved in facial recognition. It's certainly a possibility that you are experiencing prosopagnosia. It's sometimes known popularly as face blindness, although that's a very misleading term since it isn't a form of blindness at all."

Jessica frowned. This was exactly what she had focused on with her web research. She had hoped she was wrong, but now this expert was confirming her hunch.

"The term *prosopagnosia* comes from the Greek words for 'face' and 'not knowing.' It's not a problem with memory or vision or a learning disability. Our brains have a very special way of recognizing human faces that is quite sophisticated, and we believe part the area of your brain that was injured is where that processing takes place."

Dr. Nguyen continued his discussion of her condition. Her thoughts flew rapidly from question to question about what this might mean — would people believe that her "brain damage" was limited to this crazy problem with recognizing faces? What would they think at work, where her job relied on the ability to solve problems with logic and attention to a plethora of details, and to be able to present software users with well-designed *visual* interfaces.

"...wait several more months before we know if this is permanent..."

Jessica registered a phrase now and then, but her mind continued racing. Would friends and co-workers be offended if she failed to recognize them? Would she ever be able to make *new* friends?

"...support groups, particularly online..."

She recalled bookmarking several social networking groups for people who were face blind, but hadn't spent much time on those sites yet. She had been more focused on the medical and scientific information.

Jessica realized that Dr. Nguyen had stopped speaking, and was waiting for her to respond. "Sorry, I was thinking about some of the things you said..." she muttered.

"I understand. This may take some time to get used to, but I think you'll find that there are a number of strategies you can learn to help you recognize people even though you may not be processing their facial information the same way you did before. You seem quite savvy with online searches, so I suggest you follow up on that and look at the online support groups in particular. As I said, we now believe that about 2% of the population, perhaps even more, has prosopagnosia, either congenital — from birth — or like you, due to an accident or illness affecting the brain. You are still the same intelligent person as before; you may just need to develop alternative cognitive skills to compensate."

She nodded, lost in thought.

"Let's schedule a follow-up two months from now and see how you're doing by then."

Jessica returned home feeling emotionally drained. A nap was in order — doctor's orders, that is. She found it difficult to fall asleep at first as her mind raced, trying to process all the information and sort out the implications, but she drifted off at last.

***

Jessica hoped that watching a fun, light movie would lift her spirits. She picked out a romantic comedy, and set it up to watch on her big-screen TV. First, though, zap some popcorn in the microwave, pour a tall glass of iced green tea — decaffeinated, of course — and plant herself on the sofa, her legs propped on the coffee table in front of her. Pooka assumed his normal position, sprawled out along the length of her legs, facing the screen. She assumed he slept through most of the movies they watched, but he always seemed to awaken and pay attention to any scenes with animals or skiers.

Just twenty minutes into the flick, Jessie hit the Stop button on the remote. There were two actresses in the film with blonde hair, and one of them (or was it both?) sometimes pulled her hair back in a pony tail. She thought the pony-tailed actress was a third woman character until someone called her by name. Then there were the men, who all seemed to be the same guy until they appeared in a scene together. She was totally lost.

Although she had already watched it a dozen times, she switched her movie selection to *Harvey*. "Look, Pooka. It's your fellow pooka — the six foot, three-and-a-half inch invisible rabbit." She could keep track of all the characters now, even the invisible one.

CHAPTER 5

She fumbled with the handle of her briefcase as she gazed out the window of the light rail car zipping along parallel to the Interstate, bearing toward downtown Denver and her workplace. The rhythmic thump-thump, thump-thump sound of the wheels on the electric train was usually almost hypnotic, but today Jessica thought it sounded like the pounding of her heart. Her first day back at work after her accident — her "vacation." What might she expect?

She had decided to head to work even earlier than normal to avoid some of the rush hour crowding on the train. She also thought it might be good to already be at her desk when most of her co-workers arrived — she'd encounter fewer people that way, and anyone who stopped by to say hello would most likely be from her own department, offering at least that clue to their identity.

On the elevator, Jessica tried out a strategy she had read about on a face blind forum — act preoccupied with something and don't glance at anyone. No one spoke to her as she made a point of stowing her bus pass in a pocket on the outside of her briefcase, and "searching" for some unknown item there. *I dodged the bullet*, she thought as she stepped out on her floor and made a bee-line for her cubicle.

Two months ago, Jessica was delighted to be part of a change in the organizational chart of her company, DenDev Solutions. Management seemed inordinately fond of inventing new titles and shuffling roles whenever one major project was wrapped up and another was to begin. Her title — and primary responsibilities — had changed from Tech Lead to UI Senior Developer. As she explained to her non-techie friends, that translated into less heads-down, nose-to-the grindstone programming, and more user-interface ("UI") design work, an area she enjoyed and excelled at. DenDev still had independent contractors acting as consultants to meet with business clients to discuss their custom software needs. Now Jessica would play a key role in meeting with the consultant to begin designing what the software would look like to the final user. The other key player in the design phase was Jamie Rosenkrantz, Database Senior Developer. Together, they would work out how the underlying structure of the client's data would interface with the screens and reports the users would see. The specifications they produced would evolve into programming specifications, which would go to both in-house programmers and a few independent contractors if the deadlines were tight.

The best part of the new org chart was that Jessica would be working closely with Jamie. The two had discovered a true synergy when they were teamed up on a project, and had become friends outside of work. Jamie had even agreed to try out climbing with her at an indoor gym. Although he did pretty well for his first time, he declined later invitations. Jessica's suggestion that the climbing gym would provide great cross-training for his volleyball fell flat. Jamie lived and breathed volleyball when he wasn't working. He played in leagues all summer, and even managed some two-on-two "beach" tournaments at a local bar and grill with a sandy volleyball court on its patio. His teammate and life partner, Greg, shared his passion — they had met during a tournament four years ago. Indoor leagues and pick-up games at a Recreation Center dominated during cold months.

The morning passed quickly, as Jessica attacked the queue of emails, voice messages, and a surprising number of printed reports piled on her desk. *Haven't these people ever heard of a paperless office?* She had a good head start on the two-week deluge of messages, however, since she had sorted through many of them from home during the bulk of her vacation time spent "relaxing." A few people from her Software Development department stopped by her desk, and she was relieved to recognize each of them. Of course, these were folks she generally interacted with several times a week, including their weekly "Team Meeting." She had been particularly concerned with that Tuesday morning meeting, afraid that she wouldn't know who was who, but she realized that her ability to recognize people she knew well might still be intact. Could she be getting better? She pushed the thought aside, not wanting to get her hopes up too soon.

Jessica rolled her chair back from her desk, and spun around to look out the window. Another huge perk with her new title was being moved to a prime cubicle location at the corner of the bullpen filled with quartets of office cubbyholes. Her spot, like Jamie's new nook next to hers, backed up to the floor-to-ceiling windows that offered a breathtaking view of the Rocky Mountains. Mount Evans and Longs Peak in Rocky Mountain National Park dominated the view. The high peaks were still snow-covered, making the stark contrast between the intensely-blue sky and the white summits particularly brilliant. On a clear day like this, she could even pick out the Flatirons, rocky uplifted formations rising over Boulder. She grinned, remembering the very first time she had gone rock climbing. She climbed the Second Flatiron (the major formations were simply numbered from right to left as seen from town), and was so exhilarated by the experience that she was immediately hooked on the sport.

"Hey, Wonder Woman, welcome back!"

Her reverie was interrupted by Jamie's enthusiastic greeting. "Sorry I missed your entrance this A.M., but I had that thrilling Database Admin presentation to give. How are you, Girl? How was California?" He perched his butt on the edge of her desk, his green eyes sparkling, ready to catch up on all her news.

Jessica managed her rehearsed response. "Oh, it was great. Great weather, a fun group. We all had a great adventure."

Jamie raised an eyebrow. "So, it was...*great*." He pursed his lips, nodding. "Okay. That's really...*great*."

She hesitated. He knew her too well to let her off with a lame description of her *great* trip. He waited. "Let's go to lunch later this week. We can catch up," she said.

A smile returned to his face. "Sounds good. How's Thursday?"

"Deal."

***

Marilyn beamed as she toted the bag of Chinese carryout food into Jessica's kitchen. "You look like the Pooka who swallowed a canary," Jessica quipped. Speaking of Pooka, the tabby was doing his best to trip both women as they arranged the food and plates on the kitchen table, probably hoping to score a box of cashew shrimp.

"I'm just pleased to see you looking so much better, Sista! You know I worried about you the whole time I was off skiing."

Jessica arranged two sets of chopsticks on the table. "I kept telling you that you didn't have to call every day." She reached

30

up and gave her friend a hug. "But thanks for that. And for everything you've done."

They dished out helpings of rice and entrees onto their plates. Jessica plucked a piece of shrimp from the take-out box with her chopsticks, and delivered it to Pooka's bowl before digging into the feast. "So, how was the skiing? Was there new snow?"

"It was fantastic! We skied some great groomed trails on Grand Mesa, and had several downhill telemark days at Powderhorn." Marilyn was a magnificent telemark skier whose graceful turns always drew the attention of skiers around her. "And we stayed at a cool B & B in Cedaredge. You and I should make plans to go back there next winter. Or maybe this summer and do some hiking."

"Sounds fun. Let's plan on it."

Marilyn dished out another helping of lemon chicken. "So, what did your Mom say when you told her about your accident?"

Jessica rolled her eyes. "You've got to be kidding. She already worries about me every time I tell her I'm climbing. I didn't want her and Allan to show up in my driveway in the mansion-mobile, ready to come feed me chicken soup every day. When I talk to her, she sounds like they're *still* on their honeymoon, and I'm really happy for her. I don't want to put a damper on that."

"Sounds like she's really taken to RVing. Where are they now?"

"In the San Diego area. Tucson was getting to be too hot. They've got a long list of places they plan to visit through the end of the year, at least." Jessica smiled, glad that her mother had found someone to share her life with again, after a dozen years of living alone following Dad's death from cancer.

Marilyn set her chopsticks down and beamed at Jessica, her azure eyes sparkling with excitement.

"What?" Jessica asked, returning the smile.

"I met someone," she proclaimed. "A friend of Bill and JoEllen — I don't think you know them — was along on the trip. Great skier! He's an engineer at Lockheed-Martin. Funny, really sweet. And definitely easy on the eyes," she said with a mile-wide smile.

"And does this funny, sweet guy have a name?" Jessica asked, laughing.

"Jordan. Jordan Hawke."

"So, did you have your own room at the B & B?" Jessica asked. She winked.

"No, I just shared a room with Angela. Things haven't gotten to that point yet between me and Jordan. But —," she teased, "— there was definitely some kissing involved on the trip." Her smile was contagious.

"I'm really happy for you, Mar!"

"We'll have to go on a double-date sometime soon. Of course, that means you'll actually have to be willing to go out on a date sometime instead of spending your evenings and weekends working out or streaming movies at home." She gave Jessica an appraising look.

"Hey, I like going to the climbing gym or Rec Center. And going out to dinner, hiking or climbing with the gang. Though, I suppose you probably won't be joining us quite so often now that you've *met someone*. I do want to meet him, though."

"Jordan and I are planning to ski at A-Basin on Saturday. Do you want to come?"

Jessica shook her head. "I still want to be super careful not to do anything where I might hit my head again. They told me to wait a month before resuming climbing, so I don't want to take a chance, even wearing a helmet to ski."

"I understand. How about we get together for dinner that evening when we get back to town. I really want you two to meet."

"Okay, it's a date."

CHAPTER 6

Jessica strode down the hall to the conference room. Tuesday morning. Time to learn if she could recognize all the members of her work team.

She hesitated just before entering the room, pasted what she hoped would seem like a friendly smile on her face, and marched in, heading for her usual seat at the large conference table. Her eyes focused on each of the people already seated.

Jessica started a mental role call. Eduard Resnikov, Programmer. His rose-tinted glasses (a la Bono of U2) and bald pate made for an easy ID. Sarah McWilliams, Tech Lead — Jessica's former title. Plump, strawberry-blonde hair, freckles, green eyes. No problem.

Now she paused. She and Jamie had joked that junior programmers Josh and Seth — both in their early twenties and both sporting thin beards that outlined their jawlines — were the "skinny beard twins." Not that they'd had any trouble telling the young men apart. But now... She looked back and forth at the two of them repeatedly. One had slightly longer, darker hair. And their noses seemed a little different, although with one man turned to his left and the other facing more toward her, she wasn't even sure of any difference there.

Jamie plopped down into the chair next to Jessica's. He set his coffee in front of her so she could enjoy the aroma before passing it back. She waved her hands gently over the cup, savoring the scent as she continued her census. Their department manager, Paula Miramonte, had just arrived, and was installing herself at the head of the table. Paula was almost as short as Jessica, always dressed very professionally, and wore her long dark hair pinned up in a neat twist. Renee, the database tech, was seated next to Paula. She was a hefty woman who towered over her boss when they were standing.

Paula glanced at the clock and began the meeting, only to be interrupted by the arrival of Steve Kozerski, the contract programmer. Steve was a talented coder, brilliant, but was totally lacking in social skills.

"Ah, this must be blue-checkered shirt week," Jamie whispered to Jessica. Steve seemed to own just two shirts; both checkered. One was red and white, the other blue and white. As far as anyone could tell, he wore each shirt for a week at a time, then alternated with the other color for the following week. His ever-present can of Pepsi was in one hand; a pack of cigarettes was stuffed into his shirt pocket. He dropped a notepad and several folders noisily on the table in front of the seat he had chosen, took a swig of Pepsi, and deposited himself in a chair. Paula rolled her eyes ever so slightly, and began the meeting again.

The team reported their progress on their several projects, made notes about updated specs, and dispersed after forty-five minutes to resume work. Jessica immediately called up the Software Modification Request Forms they had mentioned at the team meeting and began updating them with progress notes, prioritization codes, and status codes. SMRFs — or "Smurfs" as the software department usually pronounced them — were used throughout the company to communicate software changes that were needed, programming bugs, and new features required for clients. Most of the software team members had a blue Smurf doll decorating their cubicle — a gift from their manager the previous year.

Although the QA department — Quality Assurance — would be the ultimate decision-makers for when a Smurf had been satisfactorily completed, one of Jessica's new duties was to sign off on the user interface design aspects of requests. She worked intently for the rest of the morning, calling up test versions of software modules, reviewing design notes, and updating SMRFs. After several hours, her eyes were becoming bleary. She rolled her chair back from the desk, stood, and stretched.

"Finally coming up for air, eh?" Jamie appeared by one of her cubby walls. "Are you planning on eating lunch today, or did someone coat your chair with super glue after the meeting?"

Jessica glanced at her watch. "Twenty till two? Wow, I had no idea. Damn, I haven't even visited *el baño* since I got here this morning."

She headed to the break room to microwave the frozen dinner she had brought from home. Jamie watched her retreat. "She's been so intense since she got back from vacation," he muttered to himself. "Something's going on."

CHAPTER 7

She covered her face with her hands. "I knew I shouldn't have looked," she moaned. Jessica had seen this sort of online lynch mob before when other climbers had been seriously injured or even killed in climbing-related accidents. She glanced at just one more post on the climbing forum, before closing the page in her browser.

The first week she had been home, she had checked for news articles mentioning her fall. At first the hits in the search engine were benign — "A 36-year-old female rock climber was injured after falling ten to fifteen feet off a popular climb in Joshua Tree National Park." No name, no information about what caused the fall.

A few days later, there were a few more detailed articles in some southern California papers, and she discovered the first mention of the accident on an online forum. As she had observed in the past, the replies started off with people offering get well wishes, but others began to ask if anyone had more details. Was the climber leading the climb and took a fall? Did something in the safety system fail?

The previous time Jessica had checked, the discussion was still split between well-wishers and speculators. Although no one had any additional facts about the event, several forum users had a wild assortment of theories on what happened. Eventually, someone — perhaps one of the Search and Rescue people — offered a few more details, again with no mention of her name or other personal identification. "Head injury" — "evacuated via litter" — "released from hospital the following day." Another user claimed to have been nearby when the accident occurred, and offered up his theory that she had "rappelled off the end of the rope" — which was essentially what happened, but didn't take into account Matt's error in setting up the rappel rope.

Jessica had taken a break from the forum at that point. But it was like a siren song, eventually drawing her back to the destruction of the discussion group.

The vultures had set in. With the anonymity of their online personas and odd user names, people calling themselves *RhymesWithOrange* or *GuruDude* wrote tirades about what an idiot the accident victim must be, and that she deserved to have fallen. Well-wishers jumped back in, pleading for civility and compassion, but were drowned out by the ranting of more and more of the vultures, tearing at one another and each trying to outdo the others with insults, sick jokes, and crude attacks.

But even the carnage of this phase of the online postings wasn't what had Jessica most upset. She didn't really take it personally, having seen the same pattern before. The message that had her so shaken was one posted by a user calling himself *ItWasntMe*. He — or perhaps she (Jessie didn't know which) — offered the tidbits that the victim's name was Jessica, she lived in Denver, and she had suffered a concussion. *ItWasntMe* went on to describe a touching scene of visiting her in the hospital and presenting her with the damaged helmet which had possibly saved her life.

Oh, great, she thought. Now someone she knew would piece together the fact that she had gone to Joshua Tree, and figure the 36-year-old female climber from Denver named Jessica was, indeed, Jessica Stein.

She hadn't checked her personal email inbox yet since arriving home from work. With trepidation, she accessed it, expecting to see a deluge of messages asking about her accident. Oddly, the only message she spotted was one from Allison addressed to each of the group that had been at Joshua Tree together. She opened the email, finding that it held a link to Allison's online photo album from their trip. That could wait.

Puzzled, but relieved, Jessica called back up the forum message by *ItWasntMe*. Checking the timestamp of the message, she realized it had just been posted online within the last fifteen minutes. She must have been one of the first people to read it. She looked more closely, and spotted an icon that indicated that *ItWasntMe* was currently logged into the forum. Quickly, Jessica fired off a private message to her mystery climbing partner, imploring him — her? — to remove her name and other personal details from the message.

She couldn't quite identify why she felt such panic about having people learn of her accident. It wasn't like she couldn't face up to having made a mistake. She pondered the question while nervously refreshing the page, waiting for either a direct response from *ItWasntMe* or an edited version of the message to appear.

Brain damage, she thought. *I don't want people to know I've suffered brain damage.*

ItWasntMe never responded. The message remained unchanged.

CHAPTER 8

"Meet me by the elevator in five?"

"On my way." Jessica straightened up the papers and folders on her desk, kicked off her low heels, and slipped into a pair of tennies she plucked from the bottom drawer of her desk. She grabbed her coat.

She and Jamie rode down 26 floors to the lobby. After neither came up with a strong preference for any particular cuisine, they opted to have lunch at a nearby food court. It was a chilly, crisp day, but the sun found its way between the tall buildings to occasionally warm their faces as they strode along 16th Street. They had opted to eat early, hoping to avoid crowds, and the food court was reasonably quiet. Jamie fetched pizza and salad from one food vendor while Jessica chose gyros, and they chose a table at the edge of the large seating area.

"Okay, Jessica," he drew out her full name dramatically. This was his "let's be serious" voice. "Something's bothering you. What happened on your vacation? And don't you dare tell me everything is *great* again."

She set down her food, took a determined breath, and looked Jamie straight in the eye. "There was an accident," she began.

He nodded, encouraging her to continue. "I took a fall — maybe ten feet or so — and got a concussion."

He could tell there was something more. He reached across the table and put his hand on her forearm. "Go on."

"It seems I may have damaged a part of my brain that involves facial recognition. I'm finding it really difficult to recognize people. But I do recognize you," she quickly added.

"I'm not sure I understand exactly. You hit your head — right?" She nodded. "And now you're having trouble seeing?"

"No, that's not it. My vision is fine. It's kind of strange, really, but there's an analogy I found on the web. Imagine you're looking at a dry streambed full of nearly-identical rocks. Now suppose I ask you to remember several specific rocks. Could you do it?"

"I suppose I could if I could study them for a while. Memorize some small feature on each of those rocks. Try to remember their locations relative to each other. Kind of like one of those games where you turn over pictures two at a time trying to find a matching pair."

Jessica shook her head. "I'm going to add another twist. I can rearrange the rocks any time. I might remove some, add new ones, turn some over. Now, could you identify *your* rocks?"

Now Jamie shook his head. "I sincerely doubt it."

She continued. "I never thought of it before my accident, but peoples' faces are really pretty much all the same. Nearly everyone you meet is going to have two eyes, two ears, a nose, and a mouth. In the same general locations. If we had to rely on memorizing faces the way we might try to memorize the appearance of a river rock, we'd have a hell of a time recognizing many people."

Jamie puzzled over this idea. Jessica went on, "I've learned that we have this amazing part of our brains which process human faces much differently than memorizing individual components, like how far apart the dark spots are on a rock, or if the rock is round or oval. We seem to see the entire face as a whole, and can even recognize each face when someone turns left or right or looks straight at us or whatever." Jamie glanced around at the people sitting at nearby tables, considering this. "I can't do it that way any more. They call it 'face blindness'."

"But you said you recognize me. And you've called other people by name at work this week."

"I think I'm recognizing people I already know by other clues: how they dress, how they walk, their voice, their hair style, their body type. Maybe I'm even picking up on specific features, like a facial mole or big ears. But I'm not recognizing faces the way most people do."

"Face blindness," he repeated.

"Right. That's the common name. The neurologist called it prosopagnosia."

Jamie frowned slightly and pulled out his phone. "Let's try something." He called up a photo album, scrolling through the pictures until he found the one he wanted. "Here, take a look. Recognize anyone?"

She examined the photo he had selected. "Oh, this must have been at your team's victory party after you won the winter volleyball tournament. I haven't seen these." She looked closer, zooming in on the faces of the people in the shot. "Well, this is obviously your team with those crazy tie-died t-shirts and the 'Volleyball Champ' ball caps..." She studied it further, scrolling from face to face. She frowned. "Are you in this shot?"

Jamie raised an eyebrow. "Yeah. Can you tell which one is me?"

"This one?" She pointed and turned the display so Jamie could see it.

"No." Her face fell. Jamie took the phone and flipped through a few more photos, stopping at one showing several of the team members along with several other people, all holding their beer steins in the air for a toast. "How about this one? Recognize anyone?"

Jessica looked again, a huge smile appearing on her face. "Now I recognize you. You're the one with his hat held over his heart." She chuckled. "Your hair looks almost white in this one. A little too much bleach that week, eh?" She looked at the photo again, and held her thumb over his white-blond, spiked hair in the picture. "But I don't think I would have known you if I couldn't see your hair."

"See if there's anyone else you recognize."

"Is Greg next to you?" Jamie and Greg often stood together for group photos.

"I think you're guessing now. Yes, he's on my right. Anyone else?"

She studied it a bit longer. "No. Who am I looking for?"

He took the phone and zoomed in on two women sitting closest to the camera. Held the screen up for her to see. "Oh, wow." She frowned. "That's me and Marilyn, isn't it. I can see her beauty mark now. And I recognize my blouse and how my hair is pulled back. Oh, wow. I thought I could recognize her so easily. And I couldn't even recognize myself if I didn't remember what I was wearing." Her eyes were moist.

"Jessie," he took her hands in his across the table. "It's okay. You're one of the smartest people I know. You're creative. You'll find ways to work with this, and your friends can help you."

"Jamie, I'm afraid if people find out about this, they'll think I can't do my job. What if I've damaged other parts of my brain too, and just haven't noticed the difference in how I perceive things? What if I really *can't* do my job?"

She looked around at the increasing crowd of people in the food court. Were they all strangers, as they now seemed? Would she recognize her co-workers out of context? How about personal friends? Family members? A man who had been sitting at the next table behind Jamie glanced at her. *Should I smile at him? Say hello?* she wondered. *Do I know him?* The man turned away and deposited his food tray and trash in a nearby receptacle, heading to the exit. *Or how about that woman? She seems kind of familiar. Or that one?* Jessica was starting to feel panic.

"Jessie, let me help. Don't get upset." Jamie turned to look in the direction she had been staring. "I don't see anyone from the office. Is that what you were trying to figure out?"

She sighed in relief. "Yeah. Thanks, Jamie."

"I've got your back. And I promise I'll even tell you if I think you're acting differently in other ways. But, I really don't think there's any problem with doing your job. I've been watching you work like a mad woman this week, and your new design specs are as great as ever. You've still got it, Girl." He looked at his watch. "We'd better get back. Are you doing okay now?"

"Much better." They wrapped up their barely-touched food to take back to their desks, and headed back outside.

***

"What's up?" He spoke quietly into his cell phone.

"I think we're going to be able to kill two birds with one stone. Have you ever heard the term 'face blindness'?"

"No...hang on." He paused as someone walked past. "Not over the phone. Meet me Sunday — the usual."

"Got it." The call ended.

CHAPTER 9

Marilyn's new boyfriend was far more than just "easy on the eyes," Jessica thought as they were seated at a table in a trendy Asian fusion restaurant. Jordan's strong jaw line and high cheekbones gave him a rugged look — complemented by his five o'clock shadow — and his sky-blue eyes and light brown hair spattered with a touch of gray seemed a perfect match for Marilyn's. In fact, the two tall, slim athletes looked like they were made for each other. Two graceful wild cats — or gazelles.

"How was the snow today?" she asked the couple, noting that they were very likely holding hands under the table.

"Great spring conditions, and the lift lines were pretty short all day. We got a lot of runs in." Marilyn gestured with her left hand, her right still occupied under the table. She glanced at Jordan with a broad smile. He returned her look. Jessica imagined she had just given his hand a warm squeeze.

"It's great to meet you, Jessie. Marilyn talks about you all the time. I was sorry to hear about your accident. You're doing okay now, I hope."

She took in a breath, feeling a moment of betrayal. But she realized she had never asked her friends to keep the accident itself a secret from anyone — that had just been an ongoing internal dialog she'd held with herself. What she did want kept secret — at least for now — was the damage done. Had she actually expressed her wishes out loud to Marilyn? Now she wasn't sure.

She looked directly at her friend, a slight question on her face. Marilyn shook her head "no" very subtly. She understood. She hadn't told Jordan about her prosopagnosia.

"Yeah, I'm fine now. Thanks for asking. It was scary when it happened, but Mar was there one hundred percent for me and got me through it. I was going to say how sorry I was that she ended up cutting her climbing trip short, but..." she smiled, and looked from one to the other. They laughed.

"Fate brought Jordan and me together," Marilyn declared, "and we have you to thank for that." She raised her water glass for a toast, and the others followed suit.

"Sacrifices must be made," Jess replied, still beaming. "Here's to fate." They clinked glasses.

It was an upbeat and laughter-filled evening. By the time they had finished dessert, Jessica felt like Jordan was an old friend, and that the three of them had always spent warm evenings like this. This skier / mountaineer / engineer was someone she already felt she could trust.

"Jordan, there's something Marilyn might not have shared with you about my accident." She looked over at her best friend, who smiled at her encouragingly. "I had a concussion, and it looks like there may be some permanent effects of that."

He focused on her, concern in his eyes. She described face blindness, again using the river rock analogy she had explained to Jamie at lunch a few days earlier.

"There's a chance I won't recognize you next time we meet. I don't want you to think I'm aloof or mad about something if that happens."

"Tell you what," he answered. "When I see you, I'll always give you some sort of signal so you know who I am. I could pull my earlobe," he suggested, giving his right lobe a tug. They all laughed.

"Now I'll think you're Carol Burnett!" Jessica loved watching classic TV show reruns, and immediately thought of the comedienne's signature sign off to her program.

Jordan got it; Marilyn didn't. "I'll explain it to you later," he whispered to her, a seductive tone to his voice.

"Well, I should be getting home and you two must be tired after your big ski day." It was definitely time to remember that three's a crowd. Jessica detected a subtle wink from Marilyn as they got up from the table.

CHAPTER 10

The giant TVs in the sports bar were all tuned to an afternoon Rockies game. With the warm, spring weather enticing people to be outdoors, the place wasn't as packed as usual. Two figures huddled at a table near the rear of the room, beers at hand, backs to the wall, ostensibly so they could see the screen. The older man scanned the room, alert for customers who might sit within earshot. They spoke as quietly as possible, given the volume of the game announcers.

"Inside ball, strike 2."

"I agree that she'd be right for doing the programming, but I can't believe she's going to think that I'm Covington." He ran a palm across his balding pate, smoothing hair that no longer grew there.

"From what she was saying, I think it *will* work. And we'll know before we tip our hand. Just see how she reacts when you meet her in the hallway. That'll tell us one way or another."

"Why not just do everything over the phone? I doubt she knows his voice very well — why would she?"

"No, too likely someone will hear her side of the conversation. She's no dummy; she may figure out something doesn't fit. But if she meets you in Covington's office..."

The patrons in the bar cheered loudly, drowning out any conversation. *"The Rockies have taken the lead, 3 to 2, bottom of the 5th inning."*

The room volume returned to a low din. "Okay, we can see how that plays out. If it works, I like the idea overall. If she suspects anything later, we can play that 'brain damage' card, like you said. Obviously, Covington will deny anything she says — he probably doesn't even know who she is." He rubbed the top of his head again. "Yeah, I like that. It gives us one hell of a smokescreen. We can dump this back on her head if anything goes wrong." A familiar, phony smile was pasted on his face.

His co-conspirator nodded, satisfied. "Covington's going to a finance conference for a few days at the end of the month. Some other hot shots in his department will be gone, too, plus his executive assistant. We can run our little experiment then."

The bar was engulfed with angry shouts and expletives aimed at the close-up image of an umpire on the giant screens. The older man rose, tossed some bills on the table, and departed.

CHAPTER 11

Jamie leaned over and swiftly wrote "J" and "S" in small letters, left-to-right, on the top of the notepad in front of Jessica. She glanced across the table. The "skinny-beard twins" had taken their places at the weekly staff meeting, Josh on the left, Seth on the right. These meetings were the easiest for her. Rarely did anyone other than the normal department members attend, and she had worked with many of them for several years. Other than the two young Gen-Y'ers, everyone had very distinctive attributes of style, dress, speech, and overall appearance to clue her in on their identities.

Other situations were trickier. If she knew in advance who would be at a meeting, she'd find time to call up the personnel bios on the company intranet. Not that she could look at an employee photo and recognize them later — but she could at least jot down broad observations about each person's appearance and try to match them up during the meeting. Unfortunately, especially with some of the women at DenDev, her note on the "long, curly brown hair" seen on a co-worker's portrait might be based on a 5-year-old photo, and the woman might turn out to have very short, red hair now. Men were even worse. Many had nondescript haircuts — or were bald. She had never noticed before how many men at DenDev were bald or heading that way.

Because so many of their projects saw Jamie and Jessica working on parallel parts of the software design — user interface and database structure — Jamie was often at hand to offer assistance. "Hey, Carlos — hey, Brenda. How's it going?" "Thanks for bringing that up, Miriam." He'd find a way to work each person's name into the discussion early in the meeting, while Jessica would inconspicuously jot down each name in a diagram laid out the way they were seated. If people were moving around, coming and going, she'd try to add another memory aid to her notes. "Yellow shirt." "Glasses." "Scar on cheek."

She also became adept at faking it. Once she arrived on any of her company's floors in the building, she smiled or nodded at everyone who made eye contact. If they said hello, she said hello back. Let them take the lead, listen for clues, and keep things vague.

This wouldn't have been so tough back when I first started here, she thought. DenDev Solutions had fewer than fifty employees when she was hired as a programmer five years ago. In the past eighteen months it had expanded rapidly, now topping 150 employees. The ever-growing and evolving organizational chart had become a multi-armed beast with new departments and levels of middle-management not needed back when they were smaller. Legal, Finance, Human Resources, Consulting Services, Application Implementation, Design and Development, Quality Assurance, Marketing — Jessica wondered if some of the departments had more than just one or two people in them. Even before her accident, several of her co-workers had commented that they encountered strangers in the hallways nearly every day, especially when they visited another section of the office space.

Jessica was shaken from her reverie as Paula Miramonte began the meeting. She was pleased to be able to report significant progress made on the design for the newest project she had been working on — a membership management system for a large national organization. Paula had complimented her on being well ahead of schedule, and the praise felt especially sweet. *I've still got it*, she told herself. *I'm good at my job, and I've still got it.*

"That was well-deserved, Wonder Woman," Jamie teased as they returned to their work area. "I told you your work is still as good as ever — maybe even better! Now it's been officially confirmed. So, when are you going to stop burning the candle at both ends?"

She beamed. "I'm starting to believe I'm going to be okay." She turned thoughtful. "With my work, anyway. I don't think the other...*thing*... is ever going to change. That's what they tried to tell me, but I kept hoping they were wrong."

"'They' being the doctors?"

She glanced around nervously, checking if anyone might have overheard. "Jamie, I still don't want anyone to know about this. You're the only one I've told at work," she whispered.

He looked her in the eye. "Let's go get some coffee somewhere we can talk."

She started to speak, but he playfully poked her with his elbow. "I know — you don't drink coffee. So, I'll get some coffee and you can smell it — how's that? Come on."

They stopped by the kitchen where Jamie poured himself a fresh cup of java. Jessica retrieved the last two pieces of banana bread which she had brought in that morning — a gift from her neighbor Della yesterday — and they found a small client meeting room that wasn't in use.

"Jessie, you're eating yourself alive trying to keep this face blindness a secret. I hate to see you tense all the time and working like there's no tomorrow."

"I don't want people to know." She shook her head emphatically. "They're going to hear 'brain damage' and think I'm incompetent. Or they'll figure I'm making the whole thing up. You've got to admit, 'face blindness' sounds pretty lame."

"Okay, I will admit that I had to go look it up and read more about it before I understood that it wasn't some kind of quack diagnosis somebody gave you. But it sounds like it's going to be a part of you from now on. I think you're going to have to accept that, and move on."

"I do accept it. I just don't want people to define me just by that. I'm still Jessica Stein. I'm the same person I was before the accident. I don't want people thinking I'm some sort of freak. There's a lot more to me than *that face blind girl*," she said with anger creeping into her voice.

"You bet there is. Being face blind isn't who you are. It's just another piece of information to describe you. But, believe me, even though it's hard at first to let people know about your secret, once you let it go, you'll find it liberating."

She jumped to her feet. "How do *you* know how I feel or what'll happen if I tell people the truth?" She crossed her arms, turned her head away.

Now it was his turn to be angry. "How do *I* know about 'coming out'? You've got to be kidding." He stormed to the door, paused. Turned back toward her. "Get over it, Jessica. No one's going to tell you you're damned to hell because you're face blind. No angry mobs are going to attack and beat you because you're face blind. Your parents aren't going to tell you they consider you dead because you're face blind, are they?" He stormed out the door.

Jessica could hardly breathe. She had never seen Jamie be more than mildly annoyed at anyone or anything. He was furious — at her. She sank into her chair, her back to the door in case anyone walked by. Her tears began quietly at first, but she collapsed into sobs, her face in her hands.

Finally able to compose herself, she cleared Jamie's cup and their plates, meticulously brushed crumbs off the table, and headed to the rest room. Cool water on her face and a good deal of nose-blowing got her ready to face the world again. She advanced nervously to her desk, watching and listening for Jamie's presence at his cubicle next door. It was unoccupied. She buried herself in paperwork, relieved that no one stopped by to talk to her for the rest of the day.

At the earliest time she thought wouldn't draw attention, Jessica changed shoes, donned her coat, grabbed her briefcase, and fled to catch a train back home.

CHAPTER 12

"God, I can't believe I said that to him. What an idiot." Jessica sniffed again, loudly.

Marilyn handed her another tissue, but didn't say anything. Let her get it out of her system.

"I don't even know if he was talking about stuff that happened to him personally, or to Greg, or to other people they know. Do you think Jamie's own parents wrote him off like that?" She didn't wait for an answer. "God, I go around saying that Jamie's a friend, but really I hardly know anything about him outside of work...and volleyball games."

Another tissue. Marilyn had never known Jessie to be a crier, and wondered if this was partly a lingering symptom of her concussion.

"I don't know if he'll ever forgive me. I feel terrible." Her tears had finally ended. She sipped the water Marilyn offered. Pooka had jumped onto the arm of the sofa beside her, and was staring intently at her face. He gave her a gentle head-butt to her cheek.

She managed a smile. "Thanks, Pooka. I know *you* forgive me." She picked up the cat and snuggled him against her chest. "I don't know how I'm going to face Jamie at work tomorrow."

"Maybe you should call him tonight, then."

Jessica stroked Pooka's fur, contemplating the idea. His loud purring helped to calm her, helped her gather her thoughts. She was holding an internal debate: *Call tonight? Is that too soon? If I wait, will that make it worse? What if he won't take my call?*

Marilyn recognized Jessica's indecision. "If you want me to be here with you when you call him, I will. But if you need to be alone, that's okay too."

That jolted her out of her musings. "Okay, I'm going to call him right now," she declared. She divested herself of the purring animal and gave Marilyn's arm a squeeze as she rose to go pick up the phone. "Please stay."

One ring, two, three — would he answer? Then, "Hello." She stumbled for a moment, expecting Jamie's voice but hearing Greg's instead.

"Oh, hi Greg. This is Jessie. Is Jamie there?"

He hesitated. "Oh, hi Jessie." Another pause. She heard muffled sounds, and pictured him covering the phone and whispering back and forth with Jamie. "Hang on a sec, uh...I've got something on the stove..."

Right.

She closed her eyes, inwardly reciting a newly-composed mantra, "Talk to me, Jamie. Talk to me."

"Hey, Jessie." The mantra worked!

"Jamie, I just want to tell you how sorry I am for what I said today. I don't know how I could have been so insensitive..."

"Hey, hey — it's okay. I shouldn't have been telling you that you should 'come out' *now* —only you can know when you're ready for that."

"I'm still not sure I'm ready. But you were right that I've been making this into much more than it really is. I guess I've been a real drama queen," she admitted.

"Don't say 'queen'," he said breezily — a tone she had worried she'd never hear directed to her again. She laughed. "Jessie, I just don't like to see you beating yourself up. If you're not ready to 'come out,' I'm not going to pressure you. I just know that when I came out, it was the most liberating thing I'd ever done, and probably the hardest thing I'd ever done. I don't regret it at all."

"I was just so insensitive about what you've been through. I mean, I don't even know *what* you've been through. I'm sorry."

"Hey, I forgive you. We'll talk about it sometime — but not right away."

"So, are we okay?" she asked, chewing her lip.

"Yeah, we're okay. Take care of yourself, Girl. See you tomorrow."

"You take care, too. Say hi to Greg and tell him I'm sorry I wasn't friendlier when I called — I was too wrapped up to talk to anyone but you."

Jessica set down the phone, and collapsed in relief into Marilyn's open arms for a long hug.

"Okay, drama queen. I'm heading home, but call me if you need me."

I'm so lucky to have two amazing friends, Jessica thought as she waved goodbye from her front door.

CHAPTER 13

"Come with us — it'll be good for you." Marilyn's voice was overflowing with enthusiasm.

"I don't know..."

"Jess-say," she admonished, "It's been what — six weeks? You said you haven't had a headache for weeks now, you've been getting out for long walks — it's time to climb back up on that horse, my friend."

Jessica hesitated. She hadn't climbed at all since Joshua Tree, not even at their regular indoor climbing gym. Several friends were planning on meeting there that evening after work for a few hours. She had always loved the camaraderie and the satisfaction of a fun and strenuous workout climbing on the artificial holds. Still, she was nervous.

"I just don't want to take any chances of hitting my head again. The docs were so emphatic about the effects of multiple concussions." She paced in the small area between her cubicle and the windows, grasping her cell phone tightly in her hand.

"We'll just top-rope and stay on easy routes. You know it's *extremely* unlikely that you could hurt yourself at the gym."

"I know that, but I feel like I should wear my helmet." Jessica had never seen anyone wearing a climbing helmet at the gym. "I'd look like a complete idiot."

"Hey, if you want to wear your helmet, do it. Since when do you care what people think when you're being safe? Tell you what — I'll wear my helmet, too. We'll start a new trend. Now, how about it? Are you coming tonight?"

Jessica shook her head, amazed again at Marilyn's fierce devotion to their friendship. "Okay. But I'm not looking forward to having a bunch of people asking me about the accident. That rash of emails I got after that forum post was bad enough, but by now probably everyone has heard about it. I guess we'll see tonight which ones are in the 'Matt almost killed you' camp and which ones think I'm incompetent, instead."

"Now I *really* think this'll be good for you. People care about you, Jess. That's what you're going to see."

"All right." She didn't sound convinced. "My turn to drive. Pick you up at six thirty?"

"I'll be ready. And I'll have my helmet along."

***

It seemed like Marilyn was right. Several people Jessica had climbed with before greeted her warmly when the women arrived at the gym. Marilyn had adopted the same helpful behavior as Jamie had at work, always hailing each person by name so Jessica wouldn't struggle to figure out who they were. On the few occasions when Marilyn didn't know someone, she'd step forward, hand extended, "Hi, I'm Marilyn. And you are...?" *Good thing both she and Jamie are naturally outgoing*, Jessica thought. The only comment they heard about their helmets was a compliment on the brand-new one Jessica wore — the replacement for her damaged 'brain bucket.'

"How's your knot? Marilyn prompted as Jessica tied in for her first climb of the evening. This was part of their normal routine. Even though both were experienced climbers, they knew distractions can sometimes lead to mistakes. They always checked each others' knots and harness closures before the start of every climb.

Jessica moved stiffly at first, but soon relaxed and got into the flow of motion up the easy route. When she reached the top, she glanced over her shoulder at her belayer, nodding to indicate she was ready to be lowered. Marilyn called to her, "Lowering."

Jessica was supposed to let go of her hand holds, lean all her weight back onto the top-rope, and let Marilyn begin releasing rope through her friction device, easing her down the wall. She leaned back, but couldn't bring herself to let go. Marilyn recognized Jessica's hesitancy. "Jessie, I've got you," she called up to her as she pulled the rope as tight to her friend as she could. "I've got you," she repeated. She began letting out rope once again, and this time was relieved to see Jessica's hands release as she trusted the lowering system and put her faith in her belayer. As she descended, her body relaxed and she landed softly and gracefully on her feet on the padded floor of the climbing gym, a huge smile on her face.

"Thanks for your patience, Mar. Next time, I won't need such a tight belay."

Marilyn gave her a quick hug, traded ends of the rope with her, and began tying in to climb. "If I'd had that rope any tighter, we could have played it like a banjo string. You can give me a little slack — but not like that guy over there." She indicated a young man nearby who seemed enthralled with an athletic young woman climbing on the opposite side of the gym. His hands were on automatic, feeding out rope as he belayed his partner. The rope was beginning to pile up at his feet. If his partner fell now, he'd probably hit the floor before Mr. Goggle-eyes remembered why he was standing there.

"Yo! Too much slack!" someone shouted, bringing him back to life. He quickly fed rope back through his belay device until his presence was actually useful again.

"No worries, Mar. I'll stay focused on you." They finished their knot and harness check, confirmed that Marilyn was on belay, and she danced up the route.

Jessica really got into the climbing and energetic atmosphere of the gym as the evening progressed. The two took a break after the first hour, settling into two colorful plastic chairs where they could watch others climb.

"Look, Jess, there's Matt — in the blue t-shirt." Marilyn pointed to a climber nearing the top of a difficult route. "I didn't see him come in." They watched him finish the climb and lower off. He spoke to his belayer for a moment before the other man headed off toward the bouldering area of the facility. Matt backed away from the wall, then stood and watched several other climbers for a while.

"I'm going to see if he needs a belay. I don't want him to think I won't climb with him again after J-Tree. Do you mind?"

"No problem. I want to rest a few more minutes, and I can hook up with Val or someone else if you're not done."

Jessica bounced across the padded floor to great him. Marilyn smiled, pleased to see her reach out to Matt, who still acted apologetic with everyone who knew about his role in the Joshua Tree accident. She watched as Jessica greeted Matt with a hug, and they headed over to a vacant top-rope. He smiled as he tapped the top of her helmet, then prepared to belay her. *Good for you, Jess*, she thought.

CHAPTER 14

"Jessica? Albert Covington here. Can you come up to my office?"

She sat up straighter, unconsciously pushing a stray strand of hair behind her ear as she managed to stammer, "Of course, Mr. Covington. Did you want to see me right away?"

"Yes, if you're not tied up with anything."

"No, I can be right up." She quickly saved the design document she was working on, and called up the company intranet personnel site. She brought up Covington's page, studying his photo intently. Distinguished-looking, maybe sixty-something, male pattern baldness, frameless eyeglasses. *Yep, he looks just like a VP of Finance should look*, she thought. She jumped to her feet and smoothed her slacks. Took two steps toward the hall, turned back and grabbed a notepad and pen, then strode to the elevator to head up two stories to the administrative offices. *What in the world does he want with me?* she pondered as she was delivered to the 28th floor of the building.

"She's heading toward you now. Give her another second or two...okay, go." The man kept his cell phone to his ear and stepped into the hall, turning toward Jessica who was heading toward the office he had just vacated.

"Ah, Jessica. Sorry, but this will only take a minute. I'll be right back." He gestured for her to enter the office as he hurried past, speaking into his phone as he left, "I'm on my way."

She stepped into the large office, taking in the oversized desk with an elegant nameplate declaring "Albert J. Covington" propped on the corner. Probably mahogany, she thought. Matching bookshelves filled with accounting tomes formed a backdrop to a beautiful leather office chair. She pondered sitting at one of the chairs facing his desk, but also considered the four chairs arranged at a small, round conference table on the other end of the room. Figuring that might be presumptuous, she placed herself in a leather-cushioned, straight-backed chair by the desk. While she was delighted with having a cubicle by a window, her view couldn't compare to the one from this large corner office. Mr. Covington could see everything from Pikes Peak to the south to Longs Peak to the north, not to mention having most of the city and western suburbs spread out below him.

Again, she pondered the reason for this odd meeting. Her boss was Paula Miramonte, who reported to the Director of Software Development, who reported in turn to the VP of Development. The whole Finance Department was a completely separate branch of the company. Unless they were about to redesign the organizational chart — again.

A head popped in. "Oh, sorry. I was looking for Albert..." he said, a question in his voice.

"He said he'd be back in just a minute." Jessica explained. "He headed that way," she added, pointing.

"Ah, someone got ahold of him after all. No problem. Thanks." He disappeared down the hall, and rounded a corner.

"We're good," he said quietly, with a nod as he walked past the older man. "She hasn't a clue."

"It's show time," the man said to himself as he ran his palm across his balding head and returned to Covington's office.

***

"Thanks for coming up, Jessica." He shook her hand. "Let's sit over here." They headed for the small conference table after all.

"I've heard good things about you, and that's why I'd like to see if you are available to help with a special project. We're looking at some new models for how we handle custom enhancements to our financial software. With one model, instead of having an Application Implementation Consultant install the custom software, we want to try something different in certain cases.

"Right now, we have a client who wants a new feature in their accounting system that we believe a number of other clients may want. We'd like to have one of our people in Accounting be able to simply 'switch on' this feature for any client remotely, rather than sending a Consultant out to install new software. The Consultants aren't always that versed in accounting, so having one of our own take care of it makes a lot of sense."

Jessica pondered how this might relate to her. She had done a small amount of work on the financial software when she first started with the company, but had been relieved to be moved on to projects more suited to her experience and interests. Accounting had never been her strong suit. "How do I fit in?"

He smiled. "I was just getting to that. I've cleared this with your manager, but only if this doesn't eat into your other work. I'd like you to do the programming for this experiment, but take it on after hours. DenDev can't pay you overtime, since you're salaried, but we can have the client pay you as a consultant. We've already come to an agreement with them, and can offer you $1,800 to write the code."

She raised an eyebrow. While the company health insurance had covered the bulk of her medical expenses related to the accident, co-pays, deductibles, and the like had taken a bite out of her savings. Eighteen hundred dollars would be a significant boost. However, she still had no real idea of what needed to be done, and no way to estimate how many hours she'd require to complete the task.

"Of course, I know you can't give me an answer right now without seeing the specs. But if you're willing to consider this, I'd like you to get in touch with Chase Kovac down in Accounting — do you know Chase?" He was jotting something on a piece of paper.

"I've seen the name, but don't think we've met. He's fairly new, isn't he?"

"Yes, Chase came on board with us last month. Very bright young man." He handed her the paper. "He'll go over the requirements with you, and you can decide. Here's his cell number and mine. He'll act as project manager for this, so he'll take care of passing things on for testing, and he'll do the actual implementation with the client."

He paused, giving Jessica a serious look. "Now, as I said, we are just testing out some new models for customizations of the accounting system. No decisions have been made yet on which model we'll end up using, and we've pulled some strings to be able to offer you the consultant fee.

"You are not to share this with anyone else in the company. Paula made me promise that she won't hear a peep from anyone — including you — on this, since there are a number of programmers in this company who would give their eyeteeth for this sort of assignment, and she also needs you to still give one hundred percent to your normal assignments."

"Oh, absolutely, Mr. Covington. I appreciate this opportunity, and understand the need to keep it separate from my regular duties."

"Excellent. Please let Chase know as soon as possible once you've chatted with him about the details. I've heard good things about your work, Jessica. If this goes well, it will certainly be noted in your employee file come the end of the year."

End of the year — the company euphemism for "bonus time." Jessica smiled, hoping there wouldn't be any bad surprises when she spoke with Chase Kovac.

He rose, and she mirrored him. They shook hands. "We probably won't be talking again about this project, since Chase will be coordinating everything from here on. Thanks for talking with me today."

He followed her to the door, and watched until she disappeared around the corner. He removed the reading glasses he had picked up at a drug store earlier in the week, and pocketed them as he headed down the hall to return to his own desk.

***

Jessica returned to her cubicle, thinking about Covington's offer. Moments after sitting at her desk, her office phone rang. Another internal call, she noted. "This is Jessica," she answered.

"Hey. This is Chase Kovac. Mr. Covington asked me to call and set up a time to meet after regular business hours. When do you normally leave?"

Jessica didn't know if the Accounting department had the same flex hours as Development did. "I generally finish up at four — I'm an early bird," she said.

"Can you stay a little later tonight — or is another day this week good for you?"

My only appointment this evening is with a short, furry critter, she noted. "Tonight's fine. Where do you want to meet?"

"How about the coffee shop next door at a quarter after four? I've got dark brown hair and I'm wearing tan chinos and a blue shirt."

Oh, good, she thought. *He doesn't expect me to recognize him.* "I'm short, long dark hair, and I'm wearing a purple blouse. See you then."

***

Thump-thump, thump-thump — the familiar sounds of the light rail train lulled Jessica into a tranquil mood. Her meeting with Chase Kovac had revealed a fairly straightforward programming task — one she felt confident she could complete in about eight hours. Maybe a bit less. She reviewed the arithmetic in her head again — $1,800 divided by eight hours comes to $225 dollars an hour. She beamed. And that oblique reference to the year-end bonus — icing on the already-glorious cake.

She pulled out her notes from the meeting to review them one more time. The client, an international organization with over 100,000 members, wanted to implement a special membership drive. Part of each new or renewing membership payment would be donated by the organization to a charity. The module they wanted her to write would automatically reduce the amount of money posted to the membership dues account, and post the

67

appropriate charitable amount to accounts payable. The accounting system would then issue a check to the charity.

Kovac provided her with several examples to use for testing her program. The only other piece of the task was for her to give the Accounting people a simple form to use to set up the name and address of the charity to receive the donation, and a way for them to select either a fixed dollar amount or a percentage of each membership fee to be donated. Easy-peasy.

When she arrived at her stop, Jessica virtually skipped the several blocks back to her house. She zapped a frozen dinner in the microwave and planted herself in front of her laptop. Before she began, she picked up the small framed photo on the corner of her desk. She was looking at the camera, beaming as she displayed her college diploma. Dad was beaming as well — looking at his daughter with love and pride. Jessica whispered, "You'd be proud of me, Dad."

She returned the photo to its special spot and began work on her new assignment.

CHAPTER 15

"It's supposed to be 72 degrees and sunny on Saturday. You've got to join us!" Marilyn was so excited, she was practically chirping. While climbing at the gym was fun, it couldn't compare to getting outdoors on real rock.

Jessica hesitated. She had considered finishing the programming assignment on Saturday, but decided this invitation was too appealing to pass up. "Okay, I'll go. Mar, if you get any more excited, you're going to wet yourself!"

. That didn't slow her down. "It's going to be incredible! Castlewood Canyon is such a blast. Jordan's going to join us and Allison's coming. Maybe Matt. We're going to the Castle, baby!" She starting singing "Castle on a Cloud" — off key, but with her characteristic enthusiasm.

"Stop, stop — oh, my poor ears," Jessica declared. The two were now laughing with joy.

***

The day was promising to be exactly as the weather gods had offered — cerulean blue skies with a few wispy clouds floating lazily overhead, the warmth of the springtime sun awakening the smells of new growth on the evergreens and the grasses along the trail leading up to the rock formations. The climbers had selected the east-facing cliffs which had been developed for climbing back in the '70s — maybe even earlier. There were a number of fun climbs on what was dubbed the *Grocery Store Wall*, and they were excited to discover that they had beat the crowds this morning.

Jordan had never been to the area before, so he, Marilyn, Matt, and Allison headed around one side of the formation, an easy scramble to reach the broad, flat area atop the rock face. Jessica stayed below to help them locate the correct bolted anchors for the initial climbs they had selected. She scanned the rock face, picking out climbs for the group to try as the day went on.

"Is there another anchor to your left?" she shouted when Marilyn peered over the top edge. "*Peaches and Scream* is right above me." Marilyn shifted over to the next set of anchors, and began setting up the rope, while Jessica repeated the process for Matt, who was looking for a climb called *Rat's Nest*, named for a large hole in the rock about seven or eight feet from the bottom which may have been a nest for some sort of creature at one time, but no longer seemed to offer that additional concern for the climber.

Matt made a huge point of asking if both ends of the rope he had strung from the bolted anchor were on the ground. Jessica assured him that the rope looked good from below, and he disappeared back from the edge, opting to hike back down rather than rappel. She smiled when she saw the knotted ends of the rope on the ground. When she looked up again, she noted that Allison carefully checked Matt's setup at the top before she headed down with Marilyn and Jordan.

It turned out that Jordan hadn't done nearly as much rock climbing as the rest of the group had. He explained that his main focus was on mountaineering — climbing mountains in Colorado, other parts of the U.S., and a number of technically difficult peaks in other parts of the world. To him, rock climbing was just one of the skills he needed on occasion to reach the top of a mountain, not a goal in and of itself. At Marilyn's urging, he had rented the special rock climbing shoes the group all wore for their sport. He admitted that he had only climbed using regular hiking boots in the past.

"Then you're in for a treat," Marilyn told him. "These babies are so sticky, they'll almost climb the route without you."

While Jordan didn't find that to be quite the case, he did find the climbing shoes made a huge difference, and moved up his first climb, *Rat's Nest*, with little difficulty.

"Way to go, Jordan!" Marilyn shouted with pride, and the rest of the group cheered as she lowered him to the ground beside her. Allison had started on *Peaches and Scream* with Matt belaying. Jessica had found a comfortable tree to sit against where she had a view of both routes.

"Well, that *is* a tall person's climb," Jessica quipped. She and Marilyn had a long-running joke about the merits of being tall or short for certain climbs, and Jessica figured she'd extend the ribbing to Jordan. "How tall are you, Jordan?"

"Five eleven."

"An entire inch taller than me." Marilyn informed the group. "So, my little friend," she continued, now with Jessica in her sights, "How about that lie-back over there? Now that's a short person's climb if I've ever seen one."

"I'm just saying…look at both of you. You can reach right into the Rat's Nest. I have to make about five moves before I can reach that."

The friends were having a great time, and the teasing was an integral part of the fun.

More climbers arrived. People swapped climbing routes, the stories and joking became bawdier and drew in more participants, and everyone climbed until they could barely close their hands to tie or untie a knot again. After they had pulled down their ropes, Jessica and Jordan volunteered to scramble back up to the top of the formation to retrieve the carabiners and slings that made up the anchors.

Jessica was exceptionally cautious as she worked near the edge of the cliff. Although she had often cleaned the anchors here without clipping her safety device to a bolt, this time she took no chances and chose the simplest and least exposed anchor to clean. She checked her helmet, making sure it was still firmly strapped in place. Mission completed, she crawled back from the edge as far as her safety sling would allow before unclipping it, then crawled further back before getting to her feet.

"Are you okay?" Jordan asked, observing her nervousness.

"Yeah. I'm still a little nervous, I guess, but I'm getting better." She blushed slightly, embarrassed about her timidity. "Sorry to be such a wimp."

"Don't apologize for doing what you need to do to feel safe. That sure beats the alternative."

She smiled at him, appreciating his understanding and support. He seemed like an old friend already, even though she had only known him for a few weeks.

He smiled back, pulled his right earlobe, and led the way back down to the trail.

CHAPTER 16

As she had predicted, Jessica breezed through the special programming assignment with ease, completing it by Sunday evening. Perfectionist that she was, she began thinking about issues with the new module. Had anyone thought about security concerns with this new feature? An Application Implementation Consultant would probably set up the charity and donation parameters when the module was installed, but surely they needed to password-protect the setup so an unauthorized employee at the client site couldn't change it. And, speaking of DenDev acronyms, what about creating a Smurf — Software Modification Request Form? She had logged onto the SMRF account, but her assignment wasn't in the system.

She decided to call Chase on Monday to review her concerns. After all, it sounded like he was pretty new to these aspects of the company's protocols. Jessica didn't want him to be blindsided by problems like these during his first trial as a project manager.

As he had requested, Jessica waited until she got home from work Monday evening before calling Chase on his cell. She explained her security concerns first.

"Not a problem, Jessica. I'll be the one implementing the new module you wrote, and we're just going to run it in a test environment over one weekend. If the client is happy with how the test goes, we'll go back through the usual channels and add all the bells and whistles before putting the new feature into the release version."

"So, this may be rolled out to all our clients eventually?" *That would be cool,* she thought.

"Maybe. That'll depend on what management thinks of this new model of customizing features. We'll just have to wait and see."

She was still concerned about documentation of the software feature.

"Shouldn't there be a Smurf for this?" she asked. At some point, surely an SMRF needed to be created, and her program code needed to be stored in the system, rather than just in the temporary online folder that Chase had told her to use.

"Sorry — a 'Smurf'?"

She explained the nickname.

"Oh, of course. I just hadn't ever heard it called a Smurf before."

She had the distinct impression that Chase had no idea about Software Modification Request Forms or the steps the development group normally used to track and implement software updates. But, apparently he wasn't the sort of guy who would admit when he didn't know what he was doing.

"Let me get back to you on that. I'll run your question by Mr. Covington. But I don't think we need to worry about a...Smurf... until we know if they're going to go with this plan. Meanwhile, I'll have your program tested, and as soon as we get the okay, we'll have the client cut you a check."

That sounded like a wonderful plan to Jessica.

"I think we're on track, but she seems all hung up on this Smurf thing." Kovac's voice had an angry edge to it.

"Actually, that could work to our advantage. Another trail pointing to her, if anyone really starts digging."

"I thought you said the clients would get hung up on investigating their own people — not look at DenDev as the source," Kovac was getting more worked up by the moment.

"Look, Kid. First off, most of them won't even notice anything unusual on their books, especially if we don't get greedy with any single client. Secondly, they're going to fire off an internal investigation before they even think of looking at our software. By then, we can clear the 'charity' from their system, and they'll have a hell of a time tracking that down. But if any of them ever do come back to DenDev, all roads are going to lead to this face blind chick." He smiled, running his palm along the bare skin atop his head.

"Right. So what about this Smurf? How's that going to work to our advantage?"

"Just ask her to set up a new Software Modification Request Form in the system under her name, since you haven't ever set one up before. Now there'll be an audit trail showing that she was the one who came up with the change, and even better, it solves our problem of getting her program distributed to more clients. That Smurf is going to guarantee that every single client with this DenDev module can be tapped for a 'charitable contribution.' This is going to be like shooting fish in a barrel." He sounded almost gleeful over the phone; a mood Kovac had rarely heard from him before.

"All right. I can sell that. I'll give her a call back tonight."

"How's that other piece coming along? Are you sure you know how to add that in?"

"I'm on it. I got enough out of that programming class I had to take to handle my part. My source is already done with his assignment, and doesn't suspect a thing."

"Fine. Just wait until she's totally out of the loop before you make the change."

***

A week later, Chase Kovac texted Jessica, asking to meet briefly in the building lobby at four thirty. Jessica called up his photo on the intranet, hoping to be able to recognize him again without knowing his shirt color this time. *Brown hair, maybe a couple of years younger than me.* She memorized her limited verbal description, and hoped it didn't describe too many people who might be in the lobby at the appointed time.

She opted for arriving early and pretending to be buried in a book when Chase arrived. Her plan worked — a brown-haired man, early thirties, wearing chinos and a pale yellow shirt walked directly toward her.

"Jessica, thanks for setting up that Smurf and for doing such good work on this project." He handed her an envelope as she rose from her seat. "See you around," he added, and headed out the revolving door.

She watched him depart, frowning slightly, a bit surprised at the briefness of their encounter. She sat down again, opening the envelope. Finding a check for $1,800 made out to Jessica Stein brought a smile to her lips.

Jessica decided to deposit her windfall before heading home, since an ATM for her bank was just around the corner. She filled out the deposit slip, noting that the issuer of the check was shown as "DOT Associates, Special Account" with a P.O. Box. The signature resembled claw marks Pooka might make on a cardboard box he had decided to attack. She completed the deposit, checked her bank balance, and felt eminently satisfied.

"I wouldn't mind getting a gig like that again!" she said aloud as she walked jauntily to the light rail station.

CHAPTER 17

"Mar, can you and Jordan come over to my house for dinner next Saturday? Jamie and Greg said that's a good night for them, and I really want all four of you to be there." Jessica sounded more upbeat than Marilyn had heard her since her accident.

"That should be fine — we were planning on going out Saturday night, but hadn't made any decisions on what to do. I'll check with Jordan to be sure, but I can't imagine it'll be a problem." She jotted a note on the calendar in her kitchen. "What's the occasion? You sound excited."

Jessica flipped through a recipe book as she talked. "It's a special occasion where I get to spend a fun evening with some wonderful friends who've really been there for me. We haven't gotten together with Jamie and Greg for a while, and I really want them to meet Jordan, too. It's going to be so much fun!"

"It will, indeed, Jess. Looking forward to it. But now I've got to run to my class at the Botanic Gardens. Later!"

"Knock 'em dead, Madam Professor."

***

Jessica loved cooking, but not when the meal was just for one, and not when she had just spent ten hours commuting back and forth and working. She kept the entire Saturday open for shopping for fresh ingredients for that night's dinner and preparing it.

As the dinner hour approached, Pooka stayed close at hand — or foot, to be more precise — as she worked with the items she had picked up at the Farmer's Market. She chopped fresh dill, sliced zucchini, and prepared asparagus for steaming. Jessica bribed the cat with a spoonful of sour cream in his dish to keep him from tripping her as she dipped chicken breasts in seasoned flour and began browning them. By the time the chicken broth, garlic, and dill seasoning had been added to the pan, the house was filled with delightful aromas. She would add the sour cream to the broth after everyone finished their salads.

"Did you all drive over together?" she asked when she opened the door after hearing the doorbell ring.

"Nope, we're just psychic and decided to arrive at the same time," Jamie replied.

Introductions had been made when both couples met on the front porch. Wine was poured, toasts were made to friends — new and old — and everyone made their way to the dinner table.

"Ta-da!" Jessica declared as she delivered the first two dishes of food to the table. Jordan immediately jumped up to help her bring more items.

"Jessie, this smells incredible!" Jamie proclaimed. "Not only can you cook, look how beautifully the food's arranged. You're not just Wonder Woman, you're Martha Stewart too."

Everyone laughed, and raised a toast — "To Martha!"

As they finished their meals, Marilyn made a show of looking around the table at each person, then looking at Jessica and scratching her head, melodramatically.

"What?" Jessica finally asked.

"Two..." Marilyn pointed at Jamie and Greg. "Four...," now indicating herself and Jordan. "Hmm. Someone must be missing," she said, pointing at Jessica. "Where's Jessie's date?"

"No, no, no — don't start," Jessica protested.

"Jessie and I have this symbiotic system when it comes to relationships," she continued, undeterred.

Jessica rolled her eyes and sat back in her chair. "You're going to do this, aren't you," she stated rather than asked.

"Of course. Anyway, where was I? Ah, yes. You see, when we first met twelve years ago, we were both in relationships." She gave Jessica an expectant look, waiting for her to play along.

"Oh, all right," Jessica gave a reluctant sigh, then picked up the story. "We met when we were both in a beginning rock climbing school, and hit it off right away. So, we thought it would be fun to have a double-date and figured the guys would get to be friends, too." She looked at Marilyn, who took up the story.

"The four of us went out to dinner, and..."

"...it was a disaster!" the two women said in unison.

"Why do I get the feeling that you ladies have told this story before?" Jordan commented.

"Many times before," Jamie interjected, "but go on. It gets better every time you do it."

Marilyn picked up the story again. "The guys didn't like each other at all. Then, when Mark and I got home, we started talking about how bad we thought Jessie and Tom's relationship was."

Jessica piped up, "And when Tom and I got home, we talked about what a bad relationship we thought Marilyn and Mark had."

"We couldn't figure out why they'd be together." The Greek Chorus routine again.

"Marilyn and I kept hanging out together, going to the climbing class, having lunch together, talking on the phone, getting out with new climbing friends..."

"...but we never tried to get all four of us together again. But she and I did start talking about how uncomfortable everyone was during our double-date."

"After a while — I don't remember exactly how we got around to it — we talked about what our reactions had been to each other's partner, and we both admitted that we had a lot of doubts about the relationships we were in." Jessica paused, giving Marilyn a knowing look.

Marilyn continued, "So, bottom line, we both got out of those crappy relationships, and decided we could be perfectly happy being single."

"Uh, oh," Jordan mumbled, looking very concerned.

"BUT..." Marilyn shouted, "now I've met a wonderful man, and I'm happier than I've ever been." She leaned over, gave Jordan a kiss on the cheek, and took his hand in hers. They gazed into each other's eyes, seeming to forget anyone else was in the room.

"Ahem!" Jamie cleared his throat playfully. He and Greg mimicked the other couple's body language.

"So, your point in getting me to help tell our story was...?" Jessica asked.

Marilyn tore herself away from their loving trance. "My point was: we need to find you a boyfriend. We can't let our symbiotic system get out of sync."

"Oh, oh. She's rolling her eyes again," Greg observed.

"I don't need a boyfriend. I'm happy being single. I have good friends —," she gestured around the table, "— a job I like, and I even have a cat. I don't need a boyfriend." She looked around the table, defiantly. "Besides, you know what they say. All the good ones are already taken." She smiled at Jordan. He pulled his earlobe in reply.

"Or gay," Jamie added.

"In your case, both," Jessica said.

"This sounds like a project," he replied, nodding first at Greg, then at Marilyn and Jordan. "Let's compare notes later."

Jessica moaned. "Enough, already." She stood, picking up several empty plates. "Who's ready for dessert?"

CHAPTER 18

Two figures walked rapidly along the hiking trail in the light of a sun low on the eastern horizon, enjoying the cool, crisp feel of what would pan out to be a warm June day. The petite, dark-haired woman's stride nearly broke into a run to keep pace with her lanky, blonde friend. They paused at a trail junction sign, considering which route to follow this morning. Ponderosa pines and scrub oak with fresh spring leaves lined the sides of the trails.

"You and Jordan seem so happy together," Jessica panted, glad for a few moments respite from their pace. "I still can't get over you bringing up our symbiotic relationship story in front of your own boyfriend. I think you freaked him out."

"He was fine. But you're right," she mused, "I guess we've never told that story before to anyone either of us was dating." She gestured to the right fork and Jessica nodded at her choice of paths.

Jessica tugged at Marilyn's arm before she could take off at her usual cheetah pace, signaling her to slow down. "The two of you really seem right together. You enjoy a lot of the same things, but also spend time apart from each other."

"It feels like the perfect balance for me. You know how I get when someone gets all clingy, like Mark was. Man, he always had to go with me when I went climbing, even though I could tell he really hated it. Then he started insisting I should learn to play golf with him instead of climb." She was getting worked up, and her pace sped up. Jessica jogged to catch up. "I hate golf!" she announced, eliciting puzzled glances from the man passing the opposite direction.

"Slow down!" Jessica rushed forward and grabbed her friend's arm again, this time forcing her to a stop. She burst out laughing, still holding Marilyn's arm firmly. "You've got to change the subject before you kill me."

"Sorry, Jess. I just get so worked up when I talk about that jerk."

"So, talk to me about Jordan instead. I don't think I've ever seen you happier."

"I am happy. We have so much fun together, and we can talk for hours — or enjoy just sitting quietly together reading. I love hearing his mountaineering stories, and he's always asking me to point out rare plants and show him photos and samples of my favorites."

She looked down into Jessica's eyes. "But, Jess, I don't want to neglect you and our friendship. You've got to tell me — be one hundred percent up front with me — if you're feeling like I'm not being there for you. You are still my absolute best friend, and that's not going to change."

Jessica realized, even as Marilyn spoke, that she had felt some twangs of — what? Jealousy? Fear of being left behind? Now that she let those feelings come into her conscious mind, she began to be able to let them go. "I'll tell you if I ever feel that way, Mar. But right now I just feel very happy for you." She hugged her friend.

They set off again at a gentle pace. "Oh my god!" Marilyn shouted, diving to the ground, her face propped inches above a clump of yellow flowers. "*Physaria bellii*. I found some last spring on the other end of the park, but here's another amazing specimen." She was already fumbling with her pack, pulling out her ever-present reference book and other botanist paraphernalia. She continued to rant with joy over her find, elaborating on the rarity of the plant and a data dump of everything known about it and every related species on the planet. At least it sounded that way to Jessica's ear.

Jessica laughed. "You're speaking in tongues again, Madam Professor. You know I don't speak Greek."

"Latin," she interjected as she wrote in a small notebook and pulled out her camera. "Its common name is Bell's Twinpod, and it's only found around shale outcroppings along the Front Range. Isn't it gorgeous?" she squealed. Marilyn could get as excited about a rare plant as new parents could when they first held their newborn child. "It's in the Brassicaceae Family..." She continued, her enthusiasm unabated by Jessica's near total lack of understanding what she was talking about. Jessie loved seeing her like this.

Marilyn finally decided she could abandon her find and continue with their hike. They continued in silence for a while, admiring the views of parallel hogback formations which seemed like sentries guarding Deer Creek Canyon where they were hiking. Red Dakota sandstone formations formed beautiful walls in the valley below. They came to a point along the trail where they could catch a glimpse of the Lockheed-Martin facility where Jordan worked.

"Jess?" Marilyn said, sounding hesitant.

"Yeah?" *What could this be about?* Jessica wondered.

This time it was Marilyn who stopped first. "Jordan and I have been talking about living together."

"Wow! So, how are you feeling about that?" She couldn't quite read Marilyn's expression.

She grinned, almost sheepishly. "One moment I'll think it's the greatest, most natural idea in the world, and the next moment I'll think that it's all happening too quickly."

"What's it been..." Jessica counted in her head. "Two months? Yeah, that's right. It's been ten weeks. You two met the week of my accident."

"Ten weeks. Doesn't that seem too soon to you?"

"I think it just depends on how you both feel. It's not like you have to decide today, is it?" She reached out and squeezed Marilyn's hand. "It's cool that you're even thinking about it. You'll know when the time is right."

"There is one other thing," she started, hesitantly. Her expression was a mixture of puzzlement and worry.

"Oh my god," Jessica blurted, "You're not pregnant, are you?" They had conferred many times on their common decision *not* to have children.

Marilyn covered her face with both hands, letting out a moan, and began shaking. Jessica quickly realized her friend was shaking with laughter, not tears. "What, then? Oh, man, you had me going there for a minute."

"I can't believe you thought — never mind. What I was going to say, before you started having a drug flashback or whatever the hell that was..." She had started laughing again, and had to take several deep breaths to get it together. "Okay, I was going to say that I'm concerned about, well, our age difference."

"Whose? You and me?"

Marilyn gave her a sharp look, not entirely sure if Jessica was kidding or had just lost track of the topic. "Jess, how old do you think Jordan is?"

Jessica raised an eyebrow. Marilyn probably wouldn't be asking if Jordan was in his upper thirties, which would have been her guess up until this moment. "Early forties, I guess."

"Nope. Try forty-eight. He'll be forty-nine in November."

"Wow. I'd never have guessed. Look at how fit he is — you're about the only person I know who can keep up with him. I would have guessed thirty-eight if you hadn't been hinting about your age difference."

"He's fifteen years older than me!"

"Yeah, I can do the math. So what? You two are in love, aren't you?"

She nodded.

"He's healthy and fit, you enjoy getting out hiking and climbing together, you have a great relationship — I don't think the age thing needs to be a factor at all."

She sighed, relieved at Jessica's take on the matter.

"Thanks. I told my father about Jordan, and when I told him his age, he really freaked out. Jordan's only ten years younger than Dad is."

"Well, sometimes *father knows best*, but not this time," Jessica said.

"There you go again with your old TV shows." Marilyn shook her head, amused.

"I'm surprised you knew the reference this time. You're catching on."

Marilyn glanced at her watch. "Guess we'd better head back — I've got places to go, things to do, sexy older boyfriend to see." She spun around, and sprinted back along the trail, Jessica racing to catch up.

CHAPTER 19

"If I hear one more person say 'we need the moisture' I'm going to scream." Jessica was pouting, staring out the office window. Low clouds seemed to settle around the tops of the higher skyscrapers and drops of rain snaked their way down the glass. Jamie and Sarah stood beside her and the encroaching clouds sucked away the natural light outdoors until the windows became better at reflecting the brightly-lit office around them than providing a view of the world outside. Jessica caught a reflection of Steve heading toward them, but he stopped abruptly, turned around, and disappeared into the maze of cubicles.

Sarah snorted. "Did you see Kozerski in the reflection? That guy is so weird. I always feel like he's spying on me the way he skulks around," she muttered.

"Aw, Steve's not so bad. He was probably looking for me. I have some updates to go over with him," Jessica said. "I don't think he feels comfortable approaching a group of people. I'll catch him in few minutes."

"He's only weird when it's red-checkered-shirt week. Or blue-checkered-shirt week." Jamie seemed to get a kick out of Steve's strange ways.

"I know he's odd," Jessica added, "but you've got to admit that he's a brilliant programmer." Sarah frowned. "Of course, I'd rather have someone who's a brilliant programmer," her hand gesturing toward Sarah, "*and* can interact with human beings."

"I've seen him interact with human beings," Jamie stated, hands on his hips. "Only, he needs to see them as avatars playing some online Star Wars game. That's why he's not freaked out when he talks to Jessie. She holds up her life-size Wonder Woman cutout doll, and he thinks he's talking to her avatar."

They chuckled at this, then broke up their weather-gazing turned to mirror-gazing and returned to their desks.

Jessica glanced at her cell, re-reading the text message exchange she had finished with Marilyn earlier. Plans for climbing outdoors tonight after work had been canceled ("Damn!" she had replied), but they'd head to the climbing gym instead. Jordan was going to be working late, so just the two women would carpool to the gym together.

She grabbed a folder and scanned the room for a disheveled programmer in a blue-checkered shirt.

***

"That guy's been checking you out," Marilyn said in a loud stage whisper after lowering Jessica from her climb. She tilted her head in the direction of a crowded section of the climbing wall.

"There are a dozen guys over there. Who are you talking about?"

"The one in the black 'Access Fund' t-shirt getting ready to lead that overhanging route."

"He's not checking me out. He's tying in...oh." He looked their way, smiled, then went back to tying his knot and dipping his hands into a chalk bag. "He's probably checking *you* out, Marilyn Monroe. You're the one who climbs like you're dancing ballet."

"No, it's you. You look so hot in that beautiful climbing helmet, and he's into the petite, dark-haired type. I can tell."

"You are so full of it. Are we going to climb, or stand around making up shit?"

Marilyn tied into the rope, prepared to take her turn on the route. They exchanged verbal signals and she started up the climb.

Jessica glanced over at Black T-shirt Guy as he worked his way up his more difficult route. He was a graceful climber, moving confidently up the initial section of the wall, which was perfectly vertical. She checked Marilyn's progress, then peeked back at the man. He had reached a section where the wall angled toward him, overhanging at about a thirty-degree angle. He seemed to be at a crux — the most difficult moves of a climb. He hung by his left arm, his toes barely holding his legs and lower body parallel to the overhanging wall. His brown hair was damp with sweat as he reached behind and below his hips with his right hand to grasp the rope trailing beneath him. He raised the rope up toward the carabiner dangling from a safety bolt above his head, but was unable to finagle the rope into the gate of the 'biner. His hand slipped, and he fell, arcing in a pendulum at the end of the rope as his belayer stopped his fall. He was laughing.

"Up rope!" Marilyn had moved up a couple of feet while Jessica was ogling the other climber.

She guiltily took in the slack. "Sorry. My bad!"

Marilyn was standing on two good-sized holds, obviously in a comfortable spot, looking over her shoulder at Jessica and laughing. "Enjoying the view?" she teased, nodding toward Black T-shirt Guy. Jessica blushed, and didn't take her eyes off Marilyn until she had reached the top and been lowered back to the ground.

Jessica was scoping out another climb for them to try as Marilyn finished untying from the rope. "Hi," she said to someone over Jessica's shoulder. Jessie turned around.

"Hi, I'm Sam."

Black T-shirt Guy had a great smile and warm, gorgeous eyes. Jessica spotted a small stud earring in his left ear lobe. It looked good on him.

"Hi, Sam. I'm Marilyn and my talkative friend here is Jessie."

Jessica was afraid she was blushing again. She extended her hand in greeting, "Hi." His hand was warm.

"I gotta hit the restroom — be right back." Marilyn was off in a flash, bounding across the padded floor like a gazelle. *Is this a set-up?* Jessica thought.

"Nice helmet." He nodded, not a hint of sarcasm in his voice. His eyes surveyed the room. "I don't know why we don't wear helmets more in the gym. Especially for leading. I'm going to start bringing mine."

"I just like to be cautious when it comes to my brain. It's the only one I have."

"That's smart. Can I give you a belay? My partner had to split." He indicated the man who had belayed him while Jessica was watching him climb. He had just put on a rain jacket and was heading for the front door with a small duffle in his hand.

"That would be great. I was looking at the purple route over here..." She headed to the base of a climb marked with purple strips of tape.

After she climbed and Sam lowered her, she looked around for Marilyn. She spotted her seated at one of the small tables near the entrance, sipping an electrolyte drink and chatting with some other climbers taking a break. She looked up, waved a "hello" to Jessica. Jessie pantomimed back, *Do you want to climb with us?* Marilyn signaled to go ahead without her.

Jessica took her turn belaying Sam. When he finished climbing, she looked around for Marilyn again, finally spotting her halfway up a climb across the gym. She seemed to have hooked up with a couple of other people for the time being.

"I could use a break — how about you, Jessie?"

"Good idea. I can take my pulse just by counting how fast my fingertips are throbbing."

"Let's get something cold to drink, and maybe they can give us fingerbowls to soak in."

Sam grinned. Jessica glowed back, enthralled with his smile again. They bounced over to the front counter and bought a pair of cold bottles of energy drinks. "Do you have fingerbowls?" Jessica asked the young woman behind the counter. She looked at Jessica, her expression blank. Her royal blue hair framed her head; a rainbow of face jewelry glittered under the artificial lights. She crouched behind the display counter, slid open a door, and stared intently at the array of climbing gear displayed inside.

"That's okay — never mind!" Jessica had to hold her hand over her mouth to keep from laughing out loud. Sam had already turned away, and was making funny snorting sounds, trying not to let the girl hear him laughing at her.

"I'll let you know if I see her heading over here to beat you up," Sam offered, once they were seated at a table farthest from the front counter. "Did you see the muscles on that kid? I think she works out — a lot."

"If she has a dragon tattoo and calls herself Lisbeth, let's get out of here!"

That led to talk about books, movies made from books, music, all-time favorites.

"*To Kill a Mockingbird*," Jessica declared.

"Agreed. How about non-fiction? I'm crazy about Edward Abbey."

"Oh, I love his books. *Desert Solitaire* — I bet I've read it at least four times. Have you read Craig Childs?"

"Wow — you've read him, too? *House of Rain* is wonderful..."

Favorite restaurants, places to rock climb, places to hike — the two were engrossed in their game, delighted by some oddball choice they had in common, laughing as they invented new categories.

"Favorite minute of the day."

"Favorite word beginning with 'x'."

Soon a small crowd had gathered, drawn in by their spontaneous game.

"Hey, Twinkle-Bell, I hate to break up the party, but I've got to get up for work tomorrow. Can you break away?" Marilyn stood with her arms crossed, attempting to sound stern, but fighting to keep a straight face.

Jessica rose. Sam did the same, and they headed for the cubbyhole where she had stored her street shoes and jacket.

"It sounds like the weather's supposed to clear up for the weekend. A bunch of us are heading to Boulder Canyon on Saturday. It's very good, but not my *favorite*."

"*Chocolat* — Johnny Depp," Sam interjected.

Jessica stopped, momentarily puzzled. "Oh — *Chocolat*. I forgot to list that one. Juliette Binoche and Judi Dench. Don't you love Judi Dench!" She remembered what she had started to say. "So, Saturday — climbing. Do you want to join us?"

"Sounds great." Sam fetched a pen and scrap of paper from the front counter, wrote down his phone number and email, tore the paper in two and had Jessica write her information down. "I never bring my phone when I come to the gym," he commented.

"Me, neither." She was glad to hear that he wasn't one of those people who had to stay "connected" 24/7. That drove her nuts.

"See you this weekend." She trotted to join Marilyn who was waiting at the entrance.

"That wasn't a set-up, was it?" she asked, watching Marilyn closely for a response.

Marilyn squinted through the wet windshield as the wiper blades made another swipe across the glass. "No, I swear. You read me the riot act when I tried to fix you up with JoEllen's friend, and I told you I'd cool it. That was just your own magnetic charm at work, pure and simple."

Jessica sat back in the passenger seat, smiling. "Did you check out his smile?" Hers broadened as she thought about seeing Sam again on Saturday.

She closed her eyes and imagined their next encounter. Her smile faded as she attempted to picture Sam's face. Would she recognize him when they met again? How would he react if she behaved like she'd never seen him before?

CHAPTER 20

Curiouser and curiouser, she said to herself, feeling a bit like Alice puzzling over seemingly unexplainable things happening around her.

First off, Steve Kozerski had shown up at the office today in a green striped shirt, of all things. Not checkered, not red or blue. Jessica had still recognized him easily enough, however, since his signature Pepsi can was in one hand and pack of cigarettes already adorned the pocket of his new shirt. She hadn't wanted to shake him up, so she refrained from mentioning anything about his attire.

That had been somewhat amusing. But the display on her screen right now was something else. Puzzling. Worrisome.

"See that?" He jabbed his finger at a line of the program on her screen. "*Superior_Random*. That's the randomization routine I wrote for the game he was programming."

Jessica frowned. The program Steve had told her to look at was the one she had written for Albert Covington and delivered to Chase Kovac. Someone had added one new line to her code — a reference to Steve's program that he thought would be used for a computer game.

She assured Steve that she knew nothing about *Superior_Random*, and hadn't been the one to insert it into her charitable donation program. He was explaining how he had included what he called a "hacker detection backdoor" in his software. Apparently, Kozerski was always on the lookout for other programmers who were writing gaming software and stealing his clever work. His hacker detector had alerted him to this use of his program.

Kozerski ranted on as Jessica tuned him out, focusing her thoughts on the implications of the program on her screen. Chase Kovac had asked Steve to write an unusual algorithm under the pretense of using it for a computer game he was writing for a beginning programming class. Then someone — probably Chase — had changed the donation program she wrote so that it only recorded donations randomly — about ten percent of the time.

Steve was still lecturing, now describing the intricacies of his program with dissertations on "linear congruence" and "combinatorial algorithms." Jessica tuned him out, knowing that he wasn't actually expecting a response at this point.

More puzzling than the programming change was the fact that her program had been flagged as *Approved for Release*. She called up another screen in the SMRF system. This was the worrisome part. It had gone out with the latest version release, and was installed at sixty-three client sites. The release had gone out almost a full month ago. These clients were running what was supposed to be a test — a prototype — within their *real* accounting systems.

She jumped to her feet. "Excuse me, Steve, but I've got to talk to some people about this right away." She literally grabbed him by his shoulders and pointed him away from her desk, giving him an encouraging shove in that direction. He wandered away, still expounding on mathematical theories and glancing over his shoulder now and then as he retreated.

Who to contact first? Manager of Software Development and her immediate boss, Paula Miramonte? What about the head of Implementation Services? Did any of the sixty-three clients ask their consultants to set up donation information? Were actual donation checks being sent to the charity "ABC Foundation" that she had invented to test her program?

Jessica hesitated, remembering Albert Covington's emphasis on keeping this "experiment" a secret. Now she was becoming angry. She had warned that neophyte in Accounting that they needed to follow protocol before her module could be used as anything but a test. Was it Chase who had flagged the SMRF so that it would be released to clients? She fumed. Who else *could* it be? What an idiot.

She sat back down at her desk, closed her eyes for a moment, and breathed slowly and deeply to calm herself. Her eyes popped open with a start as another thought occurred to her.

What if Chase is trying to run some sort of scam? That code to make the donations occur at random — was that done to try to keep clients from noticing that small amounts of money weren't going where they should be?

She had a dilemma. The Vice President of Finance had made it abundantly clear that she should not tell anyone else about this project. She didn't think confronting Chase Kovac would be wise — no telling how he'd react. She needed to go back to Covington with this, and let him handle it. Kovac was in the Accounting Department, after all, and Covington was his boss's boss.

She picked up her phone, and was about to enter Albert Covington's extension, when she froze. What if he's part of this, too? Or maybe I'm blowing this all out of proportion, and this was just the result of incompetence?

She placed the receiver back in its cradle. I need more information. Or evidence, as the case may be.

She headed toward Sarah's desk.

***

"Are you still able to log in to a client's computer?" Sarah had worked as an Application Implementation Consultant before her recent move into Jessica's old position, Tech Lead.

"Not any more. Why do you ask?"

Jessica had thought about her answer as she was walking over. She would tell the truth, but not get into any more detail than necessary. "I'm afraid I left some of my test code in a module I wrote for the last release. It just builds a history of transactions — a log — in a local database, but I don't want to clutter up the clients' systems with something they don't need."

She had left the test code in place intentionally, assuming it would come in handy if the program was brought up to standards later to be included in the released software. It would be removed after it had been tested by the Quality Assurance team.

"I can ask Phil to take a look for you."

"Is it possible to get me logged on? There are two different areas I need to check, and it'll take longer to give someone instructions than for me to do it myself." Jessica hoped that explanation didn't sound odd.

"Oh, sure. I'll just get the latest password from him, and then you'll be able to log in to any of our clients' systems for the rest of the week."

Jessica's jaw dropped. "Whoa. How many people have access to this password?" She realized DenDev had been playing "catch up" with development protocols and security as the company went through its growth spurt during the past year, but this sounded nuts.

Sarah rolled her eyes. "*Whoa* is right. Let's see — everyone in Implementation can access the password. And Accounting. I'm sure all the upper management can see it. Probably not Sales, and we Developers seem to be out of the loop. Oh — but get this — they do change the password every week, so our 'security' is good," she finished, sarcastically.

"Whoa."

"I'll text you as soon as I have it. Then just look for the 'Client Access' logon on our intranet. The rest is self-explanatory."

"Thanks, Sarah. This could have been really embarrassing — now I can get a fix into the system early if it turns out that I left that test stuff in there." Jessica scooted back to her desk, anxious to figure out if any clients had been making charitable donations to a bogus organization.

CHAPTER 21

Jessica grabbed her cell the moment she heard the tone indicating she had a new text message.

"pw: Syzygy"

She had already located the Client Access link on DenDev's internal system, and carefully typed "Syzygy" at the password prompt. A screen came up displaying an alphabetical list of all DenDev clients — a list that numbered in the hundreds. She saw that the list could be filtered, based on several options.

Under "Software Product" she selected "Accounting." The list shrank to one hundred seventy names. She saw that a product version number and status were listed next to each client's name, so she added a filter for version number 4.5.18 — the latest version to be released. Bingo! Now there were sixty-three businesses and organizations shown — the same total she had seen in the SMRF system. These were the clients who had the donation program she had written.

"Now what?" she wondered. She decided to click on the first name in the alphabetical list, Abada Foundation. Now she could view a cornucopia of information about the company, but she wasn't interested in their physical address and contact names.

"Here we go..." She spotted a button labeled "Client Access" — the same wording as she had used on the first screen. After a few moments, she was presented with a set of tools identical to the ones she used daily at work to access software code and databases. She nervously searched for the temporary transaction history log she had used for testing her program. *Rats! There it is.* She opened the log and found...nothing there. No bogus "ABC Foundation" donations had been created, so the client's financial transactions hadn't been affected. She let out a sigh of relief. Perhaps the control file had been cleared of her test data before it had gone out to clients.

She decided to check the control file, just in case she had missed something. She called up the form she had created for the Accounting people to set up the charity and amount or percentage to donate. Sure enough, all of her test information had been cleared. No charity name meant no donation. It looked like she had dodged the bullet. She could use the Smurf system to remove her program the next time the software was released, and no harm would have been done.

She sat back in her chair, relieved. Spinning around to face the windows by her desk, she took a moment to enjoy the view. It had turned into another bright, beautiful day, and she focused on the Flatirons, bright and clear in the distance. She let herself imagine the coming weekend of climbing near Boulder, and thought about seeing Sam again.

Turning back to her computer monitor, she closed the access screen for Abada Foundation. She was about to exit the entire system, but paused. Scanning the list of organizations with the latest software release, she noticed several of DenDev's biggest clients listed.

"I'll just check one more to be sure," she thought. She selected an Association that was probably her company's biggest client. This time, she called up the set-up form first.

She froze. Her made-up "ABC Foundation" had been replaced with another name, and all the other fields had been changed as well. Quickly, she accessed her transaction log, wondering what she might find there.

She tensed up as she scrolled through several hundred transactions. The log showed that someone had changed the donation settings several times during the month the software had been running. The charity name, however, had remained constant. She entered a command to calculate the total of all the donations shown.

"Whoa. Four thousand dollars plus change."

But, perhaps she had simply stumbled upon the client who had wanted this feature in the first place. She was still bothered about Steve's *Superior_Random* program, since it seemed odd that the client would want to set aside the donations based on random membership renewals, but she set that thought aside for the moment.

Jessica selected another large, well-known DenDev client from the list. *Oh dear.* This one showed around three thousand dollars in the log file. She saw that she could transfer selected files from the client to her computer, so she downloaded the transaction log.

Now more concerned than ever, she started back at the top of the list, copying every log she found from client sites, and jotting down a summary of what she was finding. Soon she had the sequence down pat, and finished exploring the entire list within the next half hour. She logged out of the Client Access system.

She stared at her jotted notes. Out of sixty-three clients who had installed the software update, forty-nine had her donation program enabled. She would look at the data more closely now that she had her logs readily available, but it appeared that over $90,000 had been processed through the system. In one month.

She heard her boss, Paula, talking to someone nearby. Jessica quickly stashed her written notes in her desk drawer, and pulled the notes on the application she was supposed to be working on in front of her. She'd be able to look at the logs remotely once she got home.

"Focus!" she commanded herself, and resumed her assigned work.

***

She was torn between excited anticipation and dread when she got home from work. She forced herself to attend to some normal matters such as eating dinner and feeding the cat, before she succumbed to her curiosity and planted herself in front of her laptop. Step one, she decided, was to examine the log transactions from the biggest clients more closely to try to determine what exactly was going on.

She called up the Association that she had initially thought was the client requesting the donation module.

"Where have I seen that name before?" she asked herself out loud. Pooka, who was sprawled on her desk next to the laptop, replied with a "mew."

"DOT Associates. I know that name from somewhere..." She pondered for a minute. "Of course — that was the name on the check I got for writing the software."

That was odd. Albert Covington had told her that DenDev's client would be writing her check. Why had the charity written the check instead of the client? Was this some kind of kick-back deal between the client and the charity? How did Covington or Chase Kovac fit into that scenario?

She put those thoughts on a back burner, and forged ahead.

Jessica accessed a second client's log file. Her back stiffened as she reacted in shock. DOT Associates *again*. She switched back to the first client. The address showed a P.O. Box in Cincinnati. Client number two: a P.O. Box in Chicago.

Jessica accessed several more log files as quickly as she could.

"DOT Associates ... DOT Associates ... DOT Associates!" Pooka was now staring at her, his eyes opened to their widest, the end of his tail swishing anxiously. There were several additional P.O. Boxes and cities listed, but she also started to find duplicates. It appeared that there were five or six separate addresses, but every file she opened showed DOT Associates as the payee.

If these transactions had made it through the accounting systems as she thought they had, DOT Associates had been paid $90,000 in the past month. And the money was continuing to flow.

What the hell was going on?

CHAPTER 22

Jessica rode the light rail in to work very early the next morning in a haze. *T.G.I.F.*, she thought. She was exhausted. She had barely slept the night before, trying to piece together the jumbled puzzle. The only part she felt sure of was Chase Kovac's involvement in...what, exactly? Had he seen an opportunity when Covington handed him this little project, and acted alone? Was Covington part of this? She had far more questions than answers.

She considered telling Jamie about her findings and asking for his advice. But he and Greg had left yesterday for a week-plus vacation to Hawaii. Lucky devils.

As soon as she arrived at her office, she logged in to the Client Access system again, immediately calling up the accounting records for one of the large clients that she had discovered yesterday. She needed to know if checks had actually been sent to DOT Associates. Were the funds really being diverted, as she feared, or was the data in her logs simply a dead end.

Damn. The money had been paid out to DOT Associates.

Jessica now had a few immediate issues to deal with. She needed to report this to someone. She could continue playing detective like some character in a cozy mystery novel, but this was the real deal. It seemed very likely that someone was embezzling money — DenDev and the authorities needed to be looking into this, not some programmer!

The other issue was Sarah. She was sure to ask what Jessica's research had dug up. She didn't want to drag anyone else into this or start rumors flowing, so she had practiced a vague response to give to Sarah: Yes, her test logs were still there, but no worries, she would update the SMRF system so they'd be cleaned up with the next release.

Jessica called up the internal employee information screen. She remembered that DenDev had made a big fuss about a year ago, announcing a new Fraud Hotline system. Management had acted so proud to be providing employees a way to register anonymous reports about potential fraud, ethical issues, discrimination, and the like. The buzz among employees was that the Hotline wasn't going to be used because it was administered internally. Reports went to the Human Resources Director, not to an outside investigator. Still, Jessica was relieved to have a specific way to report her findings, especially with the VP of Finance possibly involved in a fraud.

She followed the instructions on the Hotline page, filling out a simple online form. There was a space where she could fill in her name, but it was clearly marked "Optional." She thought about that for a moment, then entered her name. She felt it would be much easier to present the evidence she had gathered, show how the test log worked, and possibly even explain how the Software Modification Request Form system fed into software releases, in case the head of HR wasn't familiar with that.

She checked a box asking for a phone call in return, and provided her cell number. Clicked "Submit" and sat back in her chair feeling that a few ounces of weight had been lifted from her shoulders. A message popped up on the screen.

Thank you for using the DenDev Hotline. Your request has been submitted. Please allow up to 2 business days for a response.

She would have to wait over the weekend.

"So, how'd it go?" Jessica started at the voice behind her, and quickly closed the Hotline screen displayed on her monitor. She turned to see a zaftig woman standing by the wall of her cubicle. She had reddish-blonde hair pinned atop her head, fair skin with a dash of freckles across her nose and cheeks.

Sarah...maybe. Jessica hesitated, flustered. It was easy to assume someone with this coloring and body type was actually Sarah when she saw her sitting at Sarah's desk. Or attending a small meeting of their work team. She was pretty sure this was Sarah, but...

C'mon, Jess, she's going to think you're on drugs or something.

"Oh, hi. Sorry — you startled me," Jessica finally managed to stammer. "What did you say?"

Sarah looked at her like she was on drugs or something.

"I just wondered what you found out. With your test data...?" she prompted.

Jessica managed to recite her planned response without further stuttering. Sarah nodded, slowly. "Okay. That's good." They looked at each other in silence. Jessica wondered how much Sarah had seen before she cleared her monitor.

"Jessie, I've had this feeling for a while that something's wrong — something's been going on with you long before this test data thing. Is there anything you'd like to talk to me about?"

Later, Jessica couldn't begin to explain to herself exactly what had happened. It was like a door had been thrown open, or the sun had suddenly come out from behind the clouds. This was what Jamie had tried to tell her months ago. It wasn't like she had made a conscious decision to "come out" to Sarah at that moment, she just started telling her co-worker about her difficulties recognizing faces and ways she had found to compensate. Sarah had been puzzled by her revelation, asked a lot of questions, but seemed to accept this new fact about Jessica.

A few more ounces of stress evaporated.

CHAPTER 23

Jessica and Sam had touched base briefly by phone to confirm a meeting time and location for carpooling to climb in Boulder Canyon on Saturday. The rain had cleared out of the region by mid-week, and the day was expected to be a classic late-June, Colorado gem — sunny, warm, and dry.

She pulled into the massive Park and Ride lot and began scanning for signs of her friends. There was a group of people gathered in a rough circle near one end of the parking lot, but they were already piling into vehicles as she drove closer. Looking at their tiny daypacks and trekking poles, she figured they were off for a hike somewhere. Seeing no other people standing around outside their cars, Jessica headed to a section of the lot with a number of vacant parking places. Saturday mornings at seven o'clock tended not to be very crowded. Make that six forty-five, Jessica noted, checking her watch. Marilyn often teased her for being so obsessed with being on time that she was usually the first to arrive anywhere.

A green Prius pulled into the Park and Ride and drove slowly along its perimeter. Jessica stood behind her car, making herself visible. Could this be Sam? She realized, in dismay, that she couldn't remember anything about what he looked like other than a great smile and dark hair. The car parked in the space facing hers. She smiled at the man in the driver's seat — just in case. He nodded, then began fussing with something in the seat beside him. Was it Sam, or not? Jessica didn't want to turn away and seem unfriendly, but if it wasn't Sam, she'd seem very odd if she kept watching him.

"We're here!" Jessica hadn't heard another car approach, but knew Marilyn's voice instantly. She whipped her old silver Subaru into the space next to Jessica, and hopped out to greet her friend with a hug. A man emerged from the passenger side, and followed her over to Jessie. He tugged his right ear, then spread his arms, inviting a hug. Jessica complied, grateful for Jordan's consistent signals.

"Sam's not here yet?" Marilyn asked, looking around at neighboring vehicles, including the green Prius and the man who was now reading a newspaper as he sat behind the wheel.

"Guess not." Jessica sighed. "But that guy probably thought I was stalking him," she whispered, tilting her head in the direction of the stranger.

"Here he is!" Marilyn indicated a man in a white Prius which had just parked next to her.

At least I guessed the model of car, Jessica thought, sardonically.

Sam stepped out of his car, flashing the smile that Jessica remembered. *As long as he keeps smiling, I'm on it.*

"Turns out, we're it," Marilyn said. "Paul and Brian decided to head to Eldorado Springs instead. We can all fit in one car — I'll drive."

They piled their gear into the back of the Subaru and took off for Boulder.

***

During the ride, Jordan and Sam discovered they both were engineers — Jordan at Lockheed-Martin, Sam at Raytheon. They even knew a few people in common through their work. Jessica was pleased to learn that Sam also loved hiking, and was "working on" climbing all the Fourteeners in the state. While rock climbing was something she generally focused on during the spring and fall, she enjoyed getting up into the mountains when the hot summer months arrived and most of the snow had melted from the high trails.

The four of them enjoyed a glorious day at the crags, despite the ever-growing number of climbers who kept arriving as the day progressed. Despite? Ah, but that was another part of the joy of the sport for them — the instant camaraderie that groups of climbers often experience, even when they've never met before.

As Jessica reached the top of an especially fun climbing route, she whooped in joy. Climbing often affected her like that. When she was climbing, the only thing in her universe was the rock face around her. Work, relationships, problems — everything faded from her mind except the focus on her next hand hold, the position of her foot, the texture of the rock. And when the climb was done — whether she had reached the top or not — she reveled in the sensations surrounding her. The smell of the rock warmed by the sun, and of the trees and rotting pine needles on the ground; the intricate details of the rock and its variegated colors; the cry of a red-tail hawk circling above them; the child-like joy of watching a crow soaring *below* her. The challenge of attempting something many people couldn't even imagine trying — and the thrill when her attempt succeeded.

"Sam, there's something I want to tell you."

Jessica and Sam had found a comfortable spot to sit in the shade of some trees where they could take a break from climbing and yet have a good view of the face. They didn't want to miss any of the live action.

"Don't tell me — you're married? Gay?" Jessica was holding up her hands, signaling "stop" and laughing. He flashed his magic smile again.

"But seriously, folks..." he said, getting serious. He gestured for her to continue.

She took a deep breath. "Have you ever heard of prosopagnosia — face blindness?" It was becoming easier to start this conversation each time she did it.

CHAPTER 24

Jessica had arrived at work on Monday morning prepared to immerse herself in work — to do everything she could to keep from obsessing about what she would say to Oakley Tanner, DenDev's Human Resource Director, when he called to talk to her about her report on the Fraud Hotline. She set her cell phone close to her monitor, then did her best to focus on work. She pulled up a set of Smurfs on her screen, reviewing them carefully and accessing her design specs and the completed programs, searching for anything the programmers or testers might have overlooked.

Her eyes darted to the cell phone. *Focus!* she admonished herself. She pushed the phone to the far corner of her desk. She reminded herself that the Hotline message had said to allow two business days for a response. Friday to Monday — that's just a single business day.

Back to the task at hand. She examined each completed report and screen, checking the tiniest detail. That column heading should be nudged to the right a fraction. This font size is slightly too large. She entered notes into the Smurf tracking system, realizing the programmers who received the correction requests were going to buck at such picayune comments. She hoped to mollify them by flagging her notes as low priority. But she couldn't seem to stop herself from continuing.

Vrrrrr — Jessica jumped as her cell began pulsating on her desk. She snatched it up and answered without even glancing at caller ID. "Hello?" she said in a low voice.

"Jessica Stein? This is Oakley Tanner, HR Director. Do you have a moment to talk?"

"Uh, yes — well, I'm at my desk right now..." she said, sotto voce.

"I'd like to set a time for us to meet here in my office. Would four this afternoon work for you?"

Jessica decided the conversation could be overheard safely at this point. "That would work just fine. Thank you," she said at a normal volume.

When she hung up, Jessica sprawled back in her chair in relief. She tossed her phone into her purse where it normally resided during the work day, stood, and stretched energetically. She resumed her work, this time managing to prioritize tasks and not sweat the small stuff.

***

She stood in the doorway and rapped gently on the open door. "Mr. Tanner?"

The man sitting behind the desk pushed back his chair and stood. "Jessica. Come on in — I'll just get these out of the way." He picked up a stack of folders from his desk and deposited them atop a filing cabinet. "Please shut the door and come have a seat." He gestured to a small table in the corner of his office with two generic-looking padded office chairs facing it. Jessica thought of the luxurious versions of office furniture she had seen when she met with Albert Covington a couple of months ago. Tanner's office didn't hold a candle to the opulence of the VP's office.

"Oh, and please call me Oakley. Is it all right for me to call you Jessica?"

"Sure." She generally reserved *Jessie* for friends. She remembered when DenDev was much smaller and everyone knew each other. Back then, no one would have thought to address even the company CEO as *Mister*. She was still *Jessie* to the people who had been with the company for a long time.

"Now, Jessica, what prompted you to contact the Fraud Hotline? And remember, your report will remain completely anonymous as far as this office is concerned."

"Thank you. I appreciate that." She paused to gather her thoughts and remember what she had rehearsed in her mind. She wanted to present a concise overview of what she had learned without getting bogged down in technical details at the beginning.

"I believe I've stumbled across unauthorized programming within our latest software release. That software is skimming money from a number of our clients."

"I see. Please go on." She was surprised to see that Tanner's face was impassive. She had expected more of a reaction to this explosive news.

"I was given a programming task that was intended to be used as a test at a single client site, but someone modified my program and caused it to be included in an official software build — without my knowledge." Jessica decided not to get into how the SMRF system fed into software releases, unsure how much the HR Director knew about the technical details. *Focus on the big picture first*, she reminded herself.

"I feel certain I can identify one person who was involved in this. I also suspect at least one other, but I'm not sure if he was involved in the scam, or was blind-sided like I was." She stopped, waiting for Tanner's response. His expression hadn't changed at all — still as blank as the unmarked pad of paper which Tanner had in front of him. He was tapping his pen lightly on its blank surface.

"Jessica, can you tell me the names of these people who were involved?" He stared at her, his expression still unreadable.

Jessica's nerves were on edge. She stared into Tanner's inscrutable face, trying to commit something about his appearance to memory. The only notable feature she thought she'd remember was his bald scalp, and that wasn't very helpful considering the seeming abundance of bald men that DenDev had in management.

"Jessica? I know it can feel scary to name names, but rest assured that you will remain anonymous."

She brought her thoughts back in focus.

"I feel certain that Chase Kovac is involved in this. He's the one who was supposed to be in charge of testing my program and working with the client. It's also quite likely that he modified the program and got it embedded in the software release." She sat back in the chair, glad to have gotten that far.

"Chase Kovac — he's in Accounting, isn't he? And I believe he's only been with us a short time — perhaps two or three months." Tanner finally jotted down a few notes on his pad. "You mentioned that you suspect someone else as well..." he prompted.

Jessica adjusted her position, trying to get comfortable but failing. "The other person may have been involved in the scam, or maybe Chase just took advantage of this assignment and...the other person..." she hesitated. "This is really awkward."

Tanner gave her a forced smile. "Please, just tell me about this other person. If he — or she — didn't do anything wrong, we'll figure that out. But I need to know what you suspect so that we can investigate it further."

"Okay. Like I said, I don't know if he was involved in the scam or not, but Mr. Covington was the person who gave me this special assignment." Jessica looked for Tanner to show any shock, but he remained as detached as before.

"Al Covington? Our Finance Director?" he asked. "Why would Albert — Mr. Covington — be assigning programming projects? That seems rather unusual."

Jessica explained what she knew about the experimental model of having someone in Accounting do the actual client implementation of an accounting feature. She described Covington's emphasis on keeping her role a secret until the model had been evaluated. How he insisted that she not talk about the project with her manager, Paula Miramonte.

"Interesting. When did this meeting with Mr. Covington take place?"

Jessica pulled out her phone and scrolled through the calendar app. "That would have been April 27."

"All right." He wrote as he spoke. "Meeting with Covington, April twenty-seventh of this year. Is that right?" he asked, looking up at her.

"Yes. I wrote the program over the following weekend." She provided several other key dates when she had met with Chase Kovac.

Her narrative was interrupted by a soft, melodic sound. Tanner retrieved his cell phone from the holder on his belt and glanced at the display. "I need to take this. Excuse me just a minute..." He walked behind his desk and retrieved some papers from the center drawer. "That's excellent news. Call Richard and let him know his candidate accepted the offer."

Jessica looked around the office as Tanner continued with his call, tuning him out. That was a skill many programmers developed from working in an open area like hers, full of distracting conversations and phone calls — the ability to totally ignore voices around them when they were of no pertinence to the task at hand. She wanted to get a sense of what sort of guy this Oakley Tanner was.

To her left, she studied Tanner's "Ego Wall" — an arrangement of plaques, awards, degrees, and other accolades to his professional career. Several Associations related to Human Resource Management had provided suitably businesslike certificates with Oakley Tanner beautifully written in calligraphic style. Another framed certificate announced his Human Resource Management degree from a college in Illinois.

She looked at that one again, her attention drawn to the name on the diploma — Donald Oakley Tanner. *So, Oakley is actually his middle name.* She wondered if anyone called him Donald. Did he sign his name as "D. O. Tanner?" she thought, idly.

Then she realized Tanner's initials were D.O.T. Her eyes widened, and she quickly glanced his way, checking that he was still focused on his call. Donald Oakley Tanner — was this a bizarre coincidence, or was Tanner part of the mysterious DOT Associates?

"Sorry about the interruption, Jessica." Tanner moved back to the tiny conference table. "We're bringing in a top-notch marketing exec, and I had some things that needed to be handled right away to clinch the deal." He was looking quite pleased with himself, showing far more animation than she had thought he was capable of. "Now, where were we?" He looked at his sparse notes. "Ah, yes. You gave me some key dates of meetings with Mr. Covington and Mr. Kovac. Now, Jessica, <u>why</u> do you suspect that this — how did you word it? — *unauthorized* software is being used to skim funds from our clients? And why do you suspect Mr. Kovac of being behind this?"

She had to think quickly. Jessica wasn't certain that Tanner was part of DOT Associates, but it seemed too likely for comfort.

"Well, it's just that no one else knew about the project but Chase and Mr. Covington. Mr. Covington wasn't involved after that first meeting, as far as I could tell. But maybe he didn't understand the ramifications of what he did."

"I see. But why do you believe the software is skimming money from clients?"

She adopted what she hoped looked like a rueful expression. "Mr. Tanner, now that I've heard myself say all this out loud, I'm beginning to realize that I probably just have a vivid imagination. It occurred to me that someone *could* use this program to pull money out of a client's receivables, but now that I think about it, that doesn't make sense. An accounting department would catch something like this right away. If a percentage of every membership renewal is going into a special account, they'd be out of balance by a large amount every day. They couldn't miss it."

Except that Superior_Random ensures that the bogus "donations" happen rarely enough and the individual transactions are small enough that they'll probably chalk up the tiny differences to human error, she thought.

Tanner actually smiled. "That's all right, Jessica. I'm glad you decided to report your concerns. Better safe than sorry — right?"

She nodded, the relief on her face due to Tanner buying her story.

He studied her expression for a moment. Tanner ran a hand across the top of his bald head, then sat back in his chair.

"I'll have a talk with Mr. Kovac, however, since it sounds like he may have overstepped his authority. Is there anything else?"

"No — thank you for your understanding. I'm sorry to have taken up so much of your time," she gushed. *Don't overact, Jess,* she told herself.

"Not at all. Thank you for contacting me. It's been a pleasure." He rose, signaling the end of the meeting. Jessica popped to her feet, quickly shook his outstretched hand, and headed out of his office.

She rushed down the hall and into an elevator, her mind racing. DOT Associates. Donald Oakley Tanner.

There was something about his whole persona — the way he talked, his voice, his mannerisms — that felt...wrong. He reminded her of someone, but she couldn't think of who that might be.

CHAPTER 25

Tanner sat behind his desk, his back turned to the room, staring at nothing in particular through the floor-to-ceiling windows of his office. Jessica Stein had backed off from her suspicions — for now. Would she let it go for good?

He couldn't take that chance. Richard De Graaf, the company founder and CEO, always received a notification when a new report was entered into the Fraud Hotline database. All he'd know at this point was that Jessica Stein had initiated a complaint, and that Tanner had scheduled a meeting with her today. De Graaf would expect Tanner to update the status of the complaint within the next few days. He could mark it as *Withdrawn*, but thought De Graaf might question him on that. Or talk directly to Jessica — he wouldn't put it past him. The CEO had often spoken highly of her — she had been with the company back when it was much smaller and De Graaf had much more of a hands-on, day-to-day role.

No, he wouldn't report that Jessica had withdrawn her complaint. *Resolved*? He'd need to document disciplinary action against Kovac, and he hadn't decided what he wanted to do with him yet. *Under Investigation*? Yes. Shut it down.

It's like poker, Tanner thought. Don't get greedy. If you stay in, trying to win just one more big pot, you'll probably get burned. As the man says, you gotta know when to fold 'em.

He picked up his desk phone, punching in a four-digit extension.

"My office — now!" he barked, slamming the phone back into its cradle.

During the few minutes before Kovac arrived, Tanner's outward appearance had returned to impenetrable. "Close the door," he stated calmly as Kovac entered.

"What's up?" the younger man asked, trying to sound cool and detached, but with a hint of fear in his voice. He flopped into one of the chairs facing Tanner's desk, slouched casually, and sat spread-eagled, bouncing one foot as though he was listening to music.

"Shut it down. Tonight. All of it."

Kovac stopped bouncing. He sat up straight. "What happened?"

"That bitch followed up on you and figured out that you got her program sent out to the clients, that's what happened. Now get back to your desk and clear out all that set-up data — all of it."

"Hold on a minute. What, exactly, does she know? We've got twenty 'G's rolling in a week..."

"She knows enough to figure out you're dirty. Right now, I've got her thinking you're just incompetent." He snorted. "She got that right, anyway."

Kovac glared at him, but said nothing.

"When *anything* starts pointing back at the software, we'll start rolling everything back at her — this 'face blind' bullshit, her meeting with 'Covington,' the — what did she call it? —

Smurf record with her name on it. If we strike the first blow, this isn't going to come back to us."

Kovac continued to resist. "None of the clients are looking to DenDev for answers yet. They're probably just starting to go in circles with their credit card processors. We've got time."

"That doesn't matter any more. We need to shut the con down and be ready to shut *her* down."

"We should wait, man. Time is money, man — we've just got this thing rolling." He paced as he spoke, raising his voice and gesturing wildly.

"Keep it down, Kid. Get on this — now. That data's got to be squeaky clean by tomorrow, start of business."

Kovac opened his mouth to object again, but Tanner cut him off. "This isn't a game, asshole. Remember, I can shut *you* down like that," he hissed, snapping his fingers. "Right now I just need to report that we had a talk about you getting into that Smurf system and messing around. It would be easy enough for your *real* background check information to be discovered during my 'investigation' of this incident. Now, wouldn't that be interesting? I'm sure your Probation Officer would love to hear about your actions here."

Kovac stood, clenching his fists, his face a deep shade of red. "Don't threaten me, old man. You think you'll still have this hoity-toity job of yours after I tell people about DOT Associates? You want me to turn off the pipeline? Okay, fine. But we're changing the split. I'm the one doing all the work — you don't have a clue how to log in and clear those records, do you? Sixty-forty, or I leave DOT Associates in all those client records and turn you in." He emphasized his point by shoving one of the chairs across the room, where it crashed into a bookshelf.

Tanner eyed him coldly. "Are you done with your temper tantrum?" Kovac said nothing. "You're right. You might be able to tie me to DOT Associates. I'm also the only person who can access funds from those accounts. And I'm the one who can 'discover' your real background check report. No one is going to believe a word you say, especially since you'll be wearing one of those stylish striped jump suits after breaking your parole. Minimum of three years, right? I think you'll find that a state prison is quite a bit different from your little visits to the county jail."

Kovac studied him silently. He continued, "I imagine it won't be too difficult to get the word out to your fellow inmates about that rape incident..."

"She dropped charges. You can't pin that on me."

"I don't need to pin it on you, just let people know about it. That girl was too scared of you to press charges, but I'll bet that your cellmate 'Big Bubba' won't be so easy to beat up on. Your good looks will be *such* an asset in the joint, Chase," he added with a horrible smile on his face.

Kovac slumped.

"Now that we understand each other, get your ass out of here and clear those records before morning."

Kovac turned without a word. He opened the office door, then glared back at Tanner before kicking the door violently as he stormed off.

CHAPTER 26

Jessica didn't even remember boarding the light rail train for home or walking back to her house from the station. Her thoughts were darting around like a wild animal locked in a cage, desperately searching for release.

Whom could she trust? The Human Resources Director could be part of the scheme. What about Albert Covington? Was the Vice President of Finance really in on this as well, or had he been blindsided by a clever plot? She had plenty of questions, but no answers.

She considered confiding in Jamie. She wasn't about to call him on his vacation in Hawaii to dump this on him. What about Paula? She considered her manager's position in the company, and realized that Paula didn't have all that much clout, and would face the same dilemma as she — who could be trusted who also had any power to do anything?

She felt like she would go crazy if she couldn't talk to someone soon.

Marilyn.

Not that her best friend could do anything about the insanity at DenDev, but at least Jessica could talk it all out with someone. Tame her wild thoughts enough so she could deduce the next step.

She paced rapidly as she waited for Marilyn to answer her call. Pooka fled under the couch, peering out at her in dismay.

"Mar — I'm so glad I got you! Are you at home? Can I come over?"

"Hey — hello to you too." Marilyn could barely get a word in as her flustered friend fired questions at her. "Okay — okay. Yes, I'm at home and yes, of course you can come over. Can you tell me what's wrong?"

"There's some really weird shit going on at work. I don't want to get into it over the phone." She finally paused for a breath. "Are you sure it's okay for me to come over — right now?"

"I told you — yes. I can even get this handsome dude wrapped up in a movie so we can have a face-to-face, just us girls."

Jessica considered this for a moment. She surprised herself by listening to her gut instead of her analytical mind, for once. "If Jordan wouldn't mind being in on our conversation, I'd like to have him there." She installed herself behind the wheel of her car, and started backing out of the garage. "I'll be there in about ten minutes."

"We'll be waiting. Drive carefully, Sista."

Jessica cleared her mind as best she could of all its turmoil and focused on driving.

***

It was nearly eleven p.m. when Jessica pulled back into her driveway. She felt exhausted but considerably calmer. The three of them had hashed over all the ideas and theories she had been struggling with, even jotting down notions on sticky notes and placing them on a work table labeled with names of all the players. Jessica had seen something like that in many of the crime movies and classic TV shows she liked to watch.

After all the debate and rearranging of sticky notes, Jessica had decided what to do next. She would go directly to the top. Richard De Graaf had started DenDev with a handful of employees eight years ago. She had come on board five years back, and Richard — yes, he encouraged everyone to call him by his first name — had been somewhat of a mentor to her. He insisted on an "open door" policy — employees could just come tap on his door without going through an obstacle course of gate-keepers. Hopefully he still felt that way.

She collapsed into bed, her mind finally slowing to a normal rate, and was asleep within minutes.

CHAPTER 27

Jessica took a deep breath and stood tall — as tall as her five-foot-nothing frame would allow — and started down the hallway from the elevators. This was her second foray this morning to the executive floor. De Graaf had several people in his office for some sort of meeting when she passed by an hour earlier. She had to gather her documents and — even more so — her nerve a second time with the hope that he wouldn't be tied up in meetings or on a conference call. Perhaps setting an appointment would have been a good idea after all.

As she passed Albert Covington's office, her eyes darted to the right, trying to catch a glimpse of the man who had set everything in motion. She caught a brief image of a balding man with glasses sitting at his desk, studying something on his computer screen. She hurried on.

Jessica stood in the doorway to De Graaf's office, and rapped lightly on the open door. He looked up from the papers on his desk, smiled, and gestured for her to come into his office. "Jessie — please come on in. Good to see you."

I recognize him! Jessica thought. She realized, however, that what she recognized was his voice. His horseshoe fringe of white hair defining his baldness, his dark-brown rimmed eyeglasses. When she focused on his eyes or nose or mouth, they just seemed like everyone else's individual features.

"Hi, Richard. Have I caught you at a convenient time to talk?" Richard De Graaf had always shunned the formality of being addressed by his employees as *mister*.

"Now is fine. Have a seat. What can I do for you?"

She settled into a comfortable leather chair across the desk from the company CEO. Jessica realized she hadn't been to De Graaf's office since he and many other top people in the company had moved up to the 28th floor of the building. While De Graaf's office was larger than she remembered Albert Covington's being, it was furnished in a very similar style, and didn't seem any more opulent than the Vice President's area.

She set a folder on the edge of the desk in front of her. "I have reason to believe that one or more employees here at DenDev are involved in skimming money from forty-nine of our clients." She paused, waiting for his reaction.

He frowned. "Jessie, we've known each other for quite a while. I know you are not the sort of person to act impulsively when it comes to important matters at work." He tilted back in his chair, staring at a point on the ceiling. He returned his focus to her. "I was aware that you contacted the Fraud Hotline recently, since you chose to provide your name. I'm notified in general terms when employees use the system, but I don't get involved in the details of any complaint unless Oakley Tanner feels that a problem goes beyond simple solutions. All I know at this point is that Oakley is investigating your report, but he hasn't asked for me to step in — yet."

Jessica sucked in a breath at the mention of Tanner's name. "To be perfectly honest, Richard, I didn't tell Mr. Tanner everything that I know. I let him believe that my only concern was with one particular employee — Chase Kovac." *Okay, this is it, Jess. Lay it on the line*, she thought.

"Richard, I have evidence that some $90,000 has been skimmed from clients." She tapped the folder. "The money has gone to an entity called DOT Associates. That's D - O - T."

After talking with Marilyn and Jordan, she had realized that her suspicions about Tanner were based on coincidence — his initials — and her gut feeling that something wasn't quite right about him. She tended to trust her intuition, but could hardly expect De Graaf to do the same without substantiation. She decided not to mention Tanner at this point.

"That name doesn't ring any bells. Tell me about the evidence you brought." He indicated her folder.

She opened the cover and picked up a stack of printouts showing the detail transactions captured by her software log. "Let me explain what these logs are, and why they exist."

As De Graaf flipped through the papers, Jessica described everything she could about the sequence of events. The meeting with Covington, further discussions and meetings with Kovac, creating the Smurf (De Graaf knew the slang name well), her discovery that the software had been released to clients. She told him about *Superior_Random* being added to her code. That Steve Kozerski had written the routine for a "game" Kovac was working on.

She told him about retrieving the data from sixty-three client sites, and presented additional documents showing the set-up forms. "Someone changed the test data for these clients, each one of them set up to take money from different types of transactions."

"This certainly looks serious, Jessica. I appreciate your bringing this directly to me." He flipped through several more pages, his mouth drawn into a grim line. "Is this software still running on our clients' systems?"

"I assume it is. I've already updated the Smurf status to pull it out of the next software build, but...I just didn't know who to talk to about all this. I don't know who is involved." She shook her head in frustration. "I didn't know who I could trust." Jessica looked directly into De Graaf's eyes, her expression seeming to beg for reassurance.

"I'm glad you felt you could trust me," he said, softly. "But, I suppose you figured I'd have to be insane to sabotage my own company."

They looked at each other for a moment, and both began laughing — releasing a bit of the pressure which had accumulated during their meeting.

"Thank you, Jessie. I assure you I will take action to find out what's going on here. And we're going to issue a corrected release as quickly as possible. I'll keep in touch — I'm sure I'll have more questions for you as I delve into this. Is this my copy?" he asked, indicating the printouts he had been studying.

"Yes. Thank you so much, Richard. I feel so relieved!" She rose and headed for the door. As she exited, she heard De Graaf on the phone already, ordering an emergency software release.

Jessica stepped into the elevator to return to the 26th floor and her cubicle, so she didn't hear De Graaf making a second phone call to Donald Oakley Tanner.

CHAPTER 28

Jessica was amazed at how relieved she felt after talking to De Graaf. The burden of this whole affair was now on his shoulders instead of hers. She figured she'd still be called upon to answer more detailed questions, but knowing that the top man in the company had taken her seriously was emancipating. This called for a celebration — and what better way to celebrate than to get out on the crags with friends after work?

Jessica trod up the steep switchbacks with her heavy pack but a light heart. Marilyn had dashed up ahead, her long legs and abundant energy working to her advantage. Jordan followed close behind Jessica. Paul and Brian from the Joshua Tree trip planned to show up around five thirty. She was particularly pleased that Sam was joining them as well, although he thought he might have to work late on a project.

From a distance, the rock formations along North Table Mesa looked like a decorative skirt draping off the flat-topped hill named for its resemblance to a table. South Table Mesa was its "twin" — the two mesas defining a distinctive border to the valley below. From the climbing area, someone could probably hang-glide onto the Coors Beer plant below in the town of Golden, Colorado.

The climbers followed a rough path which skirted the base of the Golden Cliffs, selecting their climbing routes and splitting up into groups of two or three. By the time dusk arrived, they would all have traded around, sometimes leaving ropes in place so others could top-rope a climb that they didn't want to lead. For some routes, a climber would scramble up a rocky gully to access the top of the cliffs, as they had in Castlewood Canyon. Unlike Castlewood, however, the access to some of the top anchors was tricky, requiring leaning far over the cliff edge to reach the bolts or other hardware to secure the rope. For these maneuvers, many climbers built themselves a temporary anchor of climbing hardware and slings so they didn't have to worry about stretching so far over the edge that they slipped and fell.

Jessica didn't feel ready to help set up or clean top anchors at North Table. The thought of hanging head-first off the cliff and reaching down to an anchor — even with a temporary anchor to keep her safe — brought a chill to her spine. As Marilyn would have said, *No Way, Jess-say!*

Jessica was untangling a rope, preparing to belay Marilyn as she climbed a popular and difficult climb called *Deck Chairs on the Titanic*. She felt a tap on her shoulder, and looked up at an attractive man with a fantastic smile. "Hey, Jessie. It's Sam," he said, re-introducing himself.

Her smile mirrored his. How wonderful that he had remembered to help her recognize him, although Jessica thought she'd always know him by that special smile. "Hey — glad you made it."

Marilyn greeted him, then pointed off to her right. "Jordan and some other friends were just finishing a route around the bend. I'm sure you can jump on their rope before they pull it.

Then come back here and give *Titanic* a go." He wished the women luck and hiked off to find the others.

"I only have eyes — for yoooo," Marilyn warbled loudly and off-key. She winked at Jessie. "I think you've been holding out on me, Sista. Those were some mighty sweet looks you were giving each other."

Jessica flashed another enormous smile. "There's nothing to tell...yet. Believe me, you'll be the first to know when there is."

"Ah, the stuff that dreams are made of. So, are we here to swoon, or are you going to put me on belay?"

"Marilyn, you are on belay," Jessica said in the most serious tone she could manage.

"Climbing, Jessica," she returned, mimicking her tone.

"Climb on, Marilyn."

As usual, Marilyn lead the route with grace and elegance. Jessica decided to challenge herself by attempting the standard start to the climb. It favored taller people who could reach the better holds, but Jessica had managed it once before. However, after several attempts, she opted for a slightly easier approach on the left, then moved over to the "true" line of the route. "Damn! I just can't manage that start!"

"You're doing fine, Jess. This thing gets smoother every year — especially the start. It's like trying to hold a greased pig."

Jessica continued to the top, her hands becoming stiff and her forearms burning with exertion. She finally tapped the anchor with one hand, letting out a "Whoop!" of joy. She dropped both arms to her side, shaking out the fatigue. "Ready to lower. I really burned myself out on that bottom part."

"Elevator going down," Marilyn replied as she smoothly fed rope, bringing Jessica back to the ground.

Jessica fumbled awkwardly with the knot on her harness. Her forearms and hands were still so fatigued she could barely grasp anything. "Can I help you with that?" Sam had returned from climbing another route.

"I'm going to see what Jordan's up to," Marilyn announced, and hurried off, leaving the two alone.

"That was subtle," Jessica laughed, watching her friend depart. She stepped close to Sam, ostensibly so he could work on the knotted rope attached to the waistband of her harness. She could feel his soft, warm breath on her forehead as he worked the knot, bending his head down so he could see his hands. She kept her head tilted downward as well, realizing that if she looked up, their faces would be inches apart.

Sam finished untying the knot, then, ever-so-slowly, pulled the rope free from her harness. She raised her head, their faces now almost touching. He softly brushed her cheek with the backs of his fingers.

"Is anyone else waiting to get on *Titanic?*" a man's voice interrupted. Jessica and Sam stepped apart.

"I'm just going to give it a shot on top-rope, and then it's all yours," Sam said to the couple who had just arrived nearby, the man carrying a rope in his arms like a package to be delivered, the woman clanking along with climbing hardware attached to her harness and slings draped over her shoulder. He produced another of his award-winning smiles in Jessica's direction, then began tying in to the rope.

***

As the light began to fade, Jessica and Sam worked close together, packing up their gear, changing into more comfortable shoes for the hike back down the trail to their cars.

"I'd love to get together with you for dinner, a movie — whatever we can come up with — but I can't do it this weekend," he said, a disappointed note in his voice. "I've got training climbs scheduled for the next several weekends. We'll be driving up to the mountains right after work on Friday nights, and getting back late on Sundays — maybe even super-early on Monday mornings."

"Well, then we'll make it sometime during next week," she answered, smiling. "What are you training for?"

"Mount Rainier in Washington. A friend and I are signed up with a guiding company to climb it the last week of July."

"Wow. I'm impressed."

"This will be the hardest climb I've ever done, but I'm really excited about it and I think I'll be ready. Jordan's already climbed it, and he's been offering me all sorts of pointers. My brother's meeting me in Seattle for a couple of days after the climb, so we'll be traveling around to see the sights, do a little hiking, stuff like that."

They donned their packs and started down the trail, settling on the following Thursday evening for dinner. Back at the parking lot, they lingered by his car. Other climbers were toting gear to their cars, shouting goodbyes across the lot, breaking out some beers to end their evening of fun. It was like one big tailgate party.

"I was hoping for a little more...ambiance," he told her, reaching to hold her hand. That smile again.

"We'll make sure to find a quieter setting for that dinner we're going to have," she said, returning the smile and squeezing his hand. She moved closer, lifting her face to his. Their lips brushed...and three young men arrived noisily at the car parked beside Sam's Prius, hooting an exuberant stream of profanity and laughter as they fished bottles of beer from the trunk of their vehicle.

"Definitely more ambiance. Hold that thought till I see you next week." Sam touched her cheek again, then entered his car.

She blew him a kiss playfully as she hurried over to join Marilyn and Jordan for the ride home.

CHAPTER 29

"Let's talk about Jessica Stein." Richard De Graaf was sitting at his desk when Tanner arrived in his office less than five minutes after Jessica had departed. He had gestured for Tanner to have a seat across from him. "I see that she filed a complaint through the Hotline, and you've flagged it as *Under Investigation.*"

Tanner nodded. "That's correct. She had a theory that someone had sneaked a program into our software that was stealing money from clients. But then she seemed to realize how crazy that sounded, and told me she just had a vivid imagination."

De Graaf was puzzled. Had Jessica shown Tanner the printouts they had just reviewed? It seemed not. "Did she explain why she thought someone was stealing money? Did she have any evidence of that?"

Tanner smiled, rolling his eyes. "She finally admitted that she had been thinking about how someone *could* skim money from clients using our software, and convinced herself that someone was actually doing it." His expression turned serious. "Unfortunately, my investigation has turned up evidence that *she* is the one who embedded unauthorized software in our latest release. It doesn't appear to have actually done any harm — yet — but it had the potential to do so." He leaned forward in his chair, looking intently at the CEO. "I have some grave concerns about Ms. Stein's behavior in recent months."

"Go on."

"I was hoping that I wouldn't have to report this," Tanner said with a sigh. "I didn't want to prejudice her supervisor or anyone else in management, and to give her the benefit of the doubt." Another sigh. "I suppose I should have come forward with this information sooner." He pursed his lips, studying his hands which he had placed on the edge of De Graaf's desk. His boss said nothing, waiting for him to continue.

"Shortly after Ms. Stein returned from her vacation in late March, an employee came to me to report something she had disclosed to him. It seems that Ms. Stein suffered an accident of some sort during her vacation — a fall, I believe — resulting in a concussion and permanent brain damage."

De Graaf sucked in his breath. "Brain damage? What happened? Did anyone know about this?" He shook his head in dismay. "How was she able to return to work so soon?"

"I don't have any more details than that — her medical records are private, of course. It seemed that she was still able to function at her job, at least to all outward appearances. But, there's another odd part to what she told this other employee. She is claiming that she can't see faces."

"Faces? I don't understand. If she's having serious vision problems, wouldn't someone have noticed? We can provide adaptive devices if she's unable to use a standard computer monitor —"

"No, that's what's so odd. She told this employee that her vision is perfectly normal when she looks at anything other than a face." He shook his head. "That's why I'm so concerned about her behavior. She seems to be...confused. Confusing things she imagines with actual events."

De Graaf silently fingered the folder of "evidence" that Jessica had brought to him. Could she have manufactured all of it? The program she had mentioned seemed to exist, but what else was real and what was imagined?

"There's one more thing." Tanner's expression was grim. "Ms. Stein told me she had been given an assignment to write this secret program during a meeting with Albert Covington."

"What does Albert say about that?"

"Actually, I didn't even bother asking him. Ms. Stein confirmed several times that her supposed meeting with Albert was on April 27 in his office. She insisted there could be no mistake on that date."

"And?"

"Albert was in New York on the 27th as a keynote speaker for a Financial Services conference. Literally hundreds of people can confirm that he was nowhere near his office on that day, or even the days immediately before and after. Several other managers accompanied him to that conference. I'm afraid she's either lying or is again having difficulties separating fact from fiction." He sat back in his chair again, feeling victorious, but keeping his face in a mask of grave concern.

"This is very troubling. Very troubling..." De Graaf's voice tapered off. He fingered Jessica's folder full of reports again. Stared at the closed cover of the folder.

"I'd like to speak with the employee who reported Jessica's accident. What's his name?"

"James Rosenkrantz." Tanner managed not to smirk at this witty invention. After all, Kovac *had* overheard her telling her friend about her injury. Why not throw the faggot into the mix?

"Jamie?" De Graaf was surprised. *Jamie?* He had been with the company since the early days, just like Jessica. The two were clearly friends as well as strong work partners. Why would Jamie report her accident to HR behind her back? That didn't sound like him. Had the two of them had a falling out?

He made a decision. De Graaf reached into the folder and pulled out just the single summary sheet listing each of the sixty-three clients and the name DOT Associates highlighted in yellow beside forty-nine of them. He held the piece of paper in front of him as if he was reviewing it carefully. Then he turned the page around and set it on the desk facing Tanner.

"Did Jessica say anything to you about these sixty-three clients? Or does the name DOT Associates ring any bells?" He watched Tanner closely.

Donald Oakley Tanner's face froze as he forced himself not to react. *Where did De Graaf get this list?* Thinking quickly, he adopted a puzzled look, and picked up the paper, pretending to study it closely. "No, she didn't mention any clients by name at all. What does this list represent? Is this something she gave you?" He furtively eyed the closed folder with concern.

De Graaf ignored his questions. "How about DOT Associates? Does that sound familiar?"

"No, can't say that it does." Tanner twisted his mouth to one side as if racking his brain over a mystery.

Richard De Graaf was known as a shrewd negotiator. One of his strongest attributes was a keen ability to observe people's reactions to proposals. To gauge emotions. To read facial clues and body language.

He had concerns about what he was reading from Tanner.

"Thank you, Oakley, for your time today. You've brought up some very worrisome points, and I plan on following up on them personally. Jessica Stein has been with us for a number of years, and I'd hate to have to let her go, but I need to see for myself whether she is still capable of fulfilling her job duties. Or if there is another position that might be more suitable, considering her...*disability*."

"Of course. And, uh, we certainly do need to be careful with how we handle her situation in terms of the *perception* of managing an employee who has become disabled. The ADA and all that..." Tanner eagerly stepped into his HR Director role, glad to move away from the awkward questions.

"Exactly. I'm going to follow up on this matter personally. I believe Jessica may be able to open up with me about what's been going on with her since her accident. You can check off the Hotline report as *Resolved* and put this matter aside." He rose from his desk, circled around to Tanner, and escorted him to the door.

"Thanks, Richard. I hope the poor young lady can get some help with her difficulties." Tanner departed, a pleased grin on his face as he headed to the elevators.

De Graaf sat in front of his computer. Something about Tanner made him feel uncomfortable. On the other hand, if Jessica had suffered a brain injury, what might that do to her behavior? Could she have made all this up? Worse still, could *she* have been using the program to steal funds? Could her brain injury somehow cause her to forget what she had done, and decide to turn in the "culprit"?

Bottom line — someone had tampered with the software, and there was a real possibility that clients had been fleeced.

He typed "Denver Police fraud investigation" into the search engine, and jotted down the phone number he found.

CHAPTER 30

"Aloha!" Jamie pulled a sweet-smelling lei over his head and adorned Jessica's neck with the colorful flowers. She turned from her desk and gasped in delight at his brilliant Hawaiian shirt adorned with black- and orange-striped fish on a deep blue background, bright green fronds of kelp floating around pale-blue bubbles. His deep tan made his bleached hair seem even lighter than usual and his green eyes more mesmerizing.

"Wow — look at you. Is this the new company dress code? I love it!"

Jamie laughed, performing a small dance that seemed a combination of the hula and a strip-tease bump. This brought a hoot from a nearby cubicle. Several members of their team came over to welcome him back from vacation and kid him about the shirt. One of the skinny-beard twins — Jessica had no idea whether it was Josh or Seth — took her by the hands and pulled her to her feet, raving about the tropical flowers making her look like a native Hawaiian. She tried to imitate a hula dancer, much to the delight and amusement of the group.

The festivities were interrupted by Jessica's desk phone ringing. People "shhh-ed" one another amidst giggles, and dispersed as she waved them off, picking up the receiver. "This is Jessica."

"Good morning, Jessica. This is Richard. Could you please come up to my office right away?"

Her mood crashed back to earth immediately. Not that she hadn't expected De Graaf to want to talk to her again, but for a few minutes here at work she had been able to put the whole scam issue out of her mind entirely. "I'll be right up."

As she headed off, Jamie reached out and touched her arm. "Is everything okay?"

"Yeah, I think it really is. I need to go to a meeting, but I'll fill you in when I get back. And I want to hear all about your trip," she added.

Before she could dash off, Jamie pointed to the lei. "Did you want to wear that to your meeting?"

"Oh my god — thanks!" She pulled the flowers over her head and started to return them to her desk. She halted, turned back to Jamie, and adorned him with the lei once more. "Later," she smiled, and hustled over to the elevators.

***

Two people — a man and a woman — were sitting before De Graaf's desk when she arrived at his door. Richard spotted her and waved her in. The pair rose as De Graaf introduced them.

"Jessica, this is Detective Freeman," indicating the strong-looking African American woman, "and Detective Fugate." Fugate was barely taller than his partner, and appeared to spend a bit too much time snacking at his desk. Both shook hands with her, and offered their business cards.

Detective Freeman spoke first. "Please, call me LaKeisha. My partner's name is a bit easier to remember — Hal." Jessica nodded and acknowledged both officers.

"Jessica, I've called in the authorities so that we can really get to the bottom of this whole affair. The detectives would like to hear your story and get as many details as possible from you. Are you all right with that?"

"Of course," she replied. "I welcome it."

De Graaf led the way to a small conference room a short distance down the hall from his office. "I'll leave you to it, then," he said, retreating from the room and closing the door behind him.

They took seats around a small, circular table in the center of the room. A fresh pot of coffee was catching its final drips from the coffeemaker on a side table. Cups and the usual accompaniments were set out. "Coffee?" Freeman asked as she got up to pour herself a cup. Jessica shook her head. Freeman doled out a cup with two sugars to her partner, and added creamer to her own. Jessica recognized the folder she had left with De Graaf sitting in the middle of the conference table.

Detective Freeman did almost all the talking. Despite her tough, stocky build, she spoke in a warm tone, encouraging Jessica to elaborate on several facets of her story. Her dangling earrings and very short-cropped black hair imparted a grace to her robust image. Whenever Jessica mentioned a person's name during her rehashing of events, Detective Fugate would ask her to spell it out as he jotted notes on a pad. Jessica occasionally glanced at him, noting that he had shaved his typical bald man's horseshoe fringe so that only a shadow of hair remained. His bushy, dark brown mustache seemed out of place in contrast to his shiny head.

"So this contract programmer, Steve —" Freeman glanced at her partner, who supplied the last name from his notes. "—

Kozerski," she added. "Why did he come to *you* when he learned that his *Superior_Random* program was part of the software package?"

Jessica described a bit more about Software Modification Request Forms, adding that her name was listed on the Smurf in question since she had created the record, demonstrating to Kovac how the system worked.

"So, Steve told you that Chase Kovac had come to him to write this *Superior_Random* program for use in a game Chase was programming?" Jessica nodded, confirming that the detective had that correct. "Kovac is a programmer?" she asked. "I thought you said he worked in Accounting."

"That's correct — he's an accountant. I had no idea he was into programming at all, but I don't think it would be unusual for someone who majored in accounting to have been required to take a beginning programming class. Maybe Steve has a better idea how much Chase understands about programming, since Chase came to him for help." She shrugged.

"You told us that you suspected fraud when you saw *Superior_Random* used within the program you wrote. But, couldn't *Superior_Random* be a legitimate piece of an accounting system?" Freeman's voice was calm, suggesting curiosity, encouraging Jessica to speculate.

Jessica considered this possibility. "I suppose, if someone wanted to create a system to select transactions in a very random manner for audit purposes, it might be useful." She paused, giving it more thought. "But that doesn't fit this application. These random transactions are generating payments to a special recipient — DOT Associates, in all these cases. Why select only a few transactions and go to such lengths to avoid any systematic selection process? No, I don't think *Superior_Random* was being used in a legitimate manner."

"And you have no idea how it was inserted in your program." She worded this as a statement rather than a question. They had already covered this ground.

"No. I also have no idea why my program was flagged to be included as part of our software release. As I said, the only people that I'm aware of who knew anything about the program existing were Chase Kovac and Mr. Covington."

The detective leaned closer to Jessica, her dark eyes intense. "Let's talk about your meeting with Albert Covington. When did that meeting take place?"

"April 27," Jessica stated without hesitation.

"You sound quite sure of that date."

"Yes, I am. I noted the meeting on my calendar..." Jessica picked up her phone, bringing up the calendar app as she spoke, "... and I can also look at the timestamp on the program I wrote starting that same evening." She held the phone up so Detective Freeman could see the entries.

"Well, Jessica, we have a problem with that. Albert Covington was in New York at a conference from April 25 through April 28. You couldn't have met with him on the 27th. Hundreds of people saw him there."

Jessica's eyes opened wide. She looked at the display on her phone, scrolled to another area and called up a note-taking app. She shook her head. "But I'm sure it was April 27." She scowled at the screen. "He called me and asked me to come up to his office. He was called away for a few minutes, but then came back and we talked about the program. He insisted on secrecy, like I told Richard — Mr. De Graaf." She looked up, her eyes dashing from one detective to the other as they silently watched her. *They think I'm lying*, she realized.

"Jessica, what really happened? You didn't meet with Albert Covington that day. Did someone really give you that programming assignment, or was it your idea?"

Jessica's mind was racing. *I know I had that meeting. I know it was the 27*th*. How could this be?*

"No, it wasn't *my* idea. I was given this assignment."

"But not by Albert Covington at a meeting on April 27th. Jessica, we need you to tell us what really happened. Was someone else involved? Are you trying to protect somebody? We need to know the truth."

"I'm telling you the truth," she said, quietly.

There was silence in the room, stretching for almost a minute. LaKeisha Freeman watched Jessica as she sat with her hands pressed to her lips, a baffled expression on her face. Her eyes were lowered, moving from side to side as she seemed to hold an internal dialog with herself. Hal Fugate stood and placed himself slightly behind Jessica's field of vision, but she was totally unaware of anything other than her own thoughts.

The detectives exchanged glances. "Excuse us a moment, Jessica. We'll be right back." Freeman and Fugate stepped outside, closing the door behind them.

After several more minutes of silent reflection, Jessica sat up tall in her chair and softly said aloud, "Okay. Logic. Analysis. What are all the possibilities?"

A telephone sat beside the coffee cups on the side table. She rose and retrieved the small, pink pad of paper and a pencil that sat by the phone, and returned to her seat. She began writing notes.

1. Covington meeting took place on 27th — he didn't attend conference

2. Covington meeting on different date

3. I imagined it

4.

She stared at her notes. Number 1 seemed impossible — unless "hundreds of people" were wrong. She crossed it off.

Number 2? She shook her head. Jessica's friends and co-workers often teased her about her meticulous notes and ability to document dates and meetings. Not that she couldn't ever make a mistake, but she had noted the meeting date, the dates she worked on the program, the dates she met with Kovac, and the date she deposited the check. All of her records pointed back to April 27. She crossed off number 2.

Number 3. This was an extremely disturbing thought. Could she be losing her mind? Had her concussion had other long-term effects besides face blindness? She slowly drew a question mark beside number 3. Stared at it.

She shook her head, and crossed off number 3.

Number 4. I met with someone else.

"Oh my god." She said out loud. Someone had tricked her into believing he was Covington. Someone had known about her prosopagnosia. But she had hardly told anyone at that point — how did they find out?

She was interrupted in her analysis as the detectives returned. They sat at the small table again, both eyeing the pink telephone message pad in front of her.

"Is there anything you'd like to tell us, Jessica?" Freeman said.

She looked straight into the detective's face. "Yes. Have you ever heard of prosopagnosia? It's also known as face blindness."

They shook their heads, again exchanging glances.

"This is going to sound like something I've made up, but please hear me out. Look it up after we're done here — you'll find out it's real. It's extremely hard for me to recognize faces. I think that meeting I had on April 27th was with someone impersonating Albert Covington. I think they knew I was face blind, and that they could get away with it." Jessica saw the expressions on the detectives' faces. "Please — I know it sounds weird, but let me finish."

They both nodded.

She launched into an explanation of the condition, again finding it easier to describe with each telling. She concluded by telling them about her accident and medical tests. "I'll be happy to sign any sort of release form so you can verify this with my neurologist, Dr. Nguyen."

Fugate stood. "Do I have this spelled correctly?" He had jotted down "prosopagnosia" and "face blind" on a piece of paper which he held out for her to see. The corners of her mouth raised slightly. "Yes, that's right." Fugate excused himself and left the room.

"I thought of one other important thing that might be very helpful, Detective Freeman," Jessica offered.

"LaKeisha," she replied. "Please call me LaKeisha."

"LaKeisha." Jessica smiled. "I was paid eighteen hundred dollars for writing that program — presumably as a consulting fee. The check I received was from DOT Associates — the same company receiving all the 'donations.' You can get a copy of my deposit from my bank, can't you?"

"Yes, but that'll go more quickly if you'll sign a release for that information as well. DOT Associates paid you." It was a statement, not a question. "Was the check mailed to your home or...?"

"Chase Kovac handed me the check when we met briefly in the lobby."

She made a few notes. "Jessica, you said you now believe someone was impersonating Albert Covington when you met with him. Do you have any idea who you really talked to that day?"

Jessica nodded slowly. "I have a guess, but there's something I'd like to look at before I send you off on a wild goose chase, LaKeisha."

"I can understand that, Jessica, but we'd rather be the ones who decide if a lead is helpful or not."

"I just want to take a look at a photo of Mr. Covington and another employee on our internal company site. I'd really like to see if there's any way I could possibly have mistaken him for Mr. Covington."

"All right. Can you do that from your phone?"

"No, I'll have to use one of the company computers. There's one in the large conference room just down the hall."

"Okay. Let's go take a look."

Jessica led the way. She logged in and called up Albert Covington's picture first. She opened a second window on the screen so she could view photos side by side.

Both men were bald, with brown hair fringing the sides of their heads. They both seemed to be in their fifties or maybe early sixties. One wore glasses. As Jessica stared intently at both photos, she could pick out some differences. One had thinner lips than the other. One had a rounder face. Their eyes were different shades of brown.

Detective Freeman had been looking at the photos over Jessica's shoulder. She noted that they were both bald and Caucasian, but could see no other resemblance between the two men.

"Jessica? What do you think? Could you have mistaken that man for Mr. Covington?"

"Yes. Especially if he was wearing glasses. I think this is the person I met with."

Detective Fugate stuck his head through the doorway. "Ah, here you are." He gestured to Freeman, and she met him in the hall. They talked quietly for a minute, then both returned.

"That's quite an interesting thing — prosopag..." he glanced at his notes, "...agnosia."

"Yeah, it's *interesting*, all right," Jessica said with a hint of sarcasm.

"And who are we looking at here?" he asked, peering at the monitor. "Oakley Tanner. Director of Human Resources."

"Jessica says she believes that is the person who met with her on April 27 and asked her to write the software."

"*Donald* Oakley Tanner," Jessica said. "His full name is Donald Oakley Tanner."

Detective LaKeisha Freeman frowned a moment, contemplating. "His initials are D - O - T. DOT." She tilted her head slightly, looking at Hal Fugate.

Fugate returned her gaze. "Could be coincidence."

"I don't care much for coincidence," she replied.

***

Jessica stole a quick glance at her watch. Almost noon — she had been answering questions for nearly four hours. She was exhausted. Fortunately, the detectives had told her she'd be free to return to her desk once she finished showing the IT tech officer from the police department how she had accessed the client records.

Richard De Graaf had logged into the Client Access system using his name and password, then had Jessica take over her demonstration. DenDev's corporate attorney had joined the meeting. Officer Tariq Singh jotted down a few notes as Jessica selected one of DenDev's largest clients, then called up the control form she had created for Accounting to set up the donation recipient and amounts.

The control form was blank.

"Let me double-check that I've got the right client," she muttered. She went through the steps again. Still blank.

"Someone's gone in and cleared this out." She turned from face to face, searching for agreement. De Graaf looked concerned. The lawyer glared at her. Singh was poker-faced. He looked at Jessica's corresponding printout showing DOT Associates as the payee, then looked at her, questioningly.

"Okay," she said, more to calm herself than anything else. "Let's take a look at the detailed transaction log that my program created. This was the code I put in when I was debugging it. Every time the charity was paid a portion of a transaction, I saved all the details in this log." She had navigated to a different screen while she was talking, and located the name of the log. Now she hesitated, afraid of what the log would — or wouldn't — show.

She smiled in triumph. "Here we go." She scrolled through screen after screen of items showing payments to DOT Associates — the same details Officer Singh saw as he flipped through the pages of printouts.

"Somebody knew how to clear the information in the control form, but they didn't know about the detail log." Singh was nodding.

Jessica looked around the room again, relieved at the change in the expressions she saw. "Let's check another client."

Singh held his hand up. "I can take it from here, Ms. Stein. Thank you for your cooperation. Unless anyone else has questions for you —" He looked at De Graaf and the lawyer, then turned back to Jessica, "— you can return to work now. I'm sure we'll need to meet with you again, but that's probably it for today."

De Graaf placed a hand on her shoulder, and gently guided her to the door. "Thanks, Jessica. I know this has been difficult, but I appreciate your coming forward."

"I hope I've helped," she managed before turning to make her way to the elevators. As she passed the conference room where she had spent much of the morning, a man with a bushy mustache and shaved head was stepping out. He closed the door behind him and nodded to her before heading back the way she had just come. She caught a glimpse of a man with spiky blond hair, his brightly-colored shirt a sharp contrast to the tans and dark burgundy colors of the room. *Jamie,* she thought, surprised. *Why would they be questioning Jamie?*

CHAPTER 31

Jessica forced herself to eat, although she didn't feel hungry. She had envisioned a fun lunch today with Jamie, looking at photos of his tropical vacation, listening to stories about parasailing and snorkeling. Instead, she was eating a cup of ramen noodles at her desk and trying to catch up on emails and calls she usually would have handled during her first hour at work. She stared at the lei Jamie had given her this morning, now draped over her monitor. That seemed like a week ago.

She popped her head out of her cubicle every time she heard the distinctive ring of calls originating within the company. Was another co-worker being summoned by the police? She had already seen Sarah leave suddenly after she received an internal call. Had the detectives talked to Kovac yet? Or Tanner? Would they be placed under arrest?

She had finally managed to immerse herself in the work she was supposed to be doing when she heard Jamie return to his desk. Noisily. He launched himself into his office chair with a thud — quite the contrast to his usual athletic grace. Jessica pushed her chair back from the desk and turned toward him. His green eyes focused on hers with an intensity she had never seen before.

"Are you okay?" she asked, hesitation in her voice.

His face was drawn, his nostrils flared. He looked away, staring toward the windows, then seemed to gather his emotions and turned back toward her.

"Jessica, you know I would never...betray you. Particularly not by going to that scumbag with something when you had confided in me." He sucked in a breath. He was gripping the arms of his chair as if he might fly away if he let go.

She jumped to her feet and rolled her chair directly in front of him. She sat, their knees almost touching, and placed a hand on his wrist. "Of course I know that. What happened? Why did they want to talk to you?"

"Jessie, what in the hell is going on?" He spoke with intensity, but kept his voice low. "Why are there detectives upstairs asking about your accident? It sounds like that HR guy Tanner claimed I told him about what happened to you. I would *never* have done that — even after we had that *thing* about 'coming out' with your face blindness. You asked me to keep it to myself, and I would never break that trust."

"I know that — Jamie, I know that!" She gripped both his wrists. "I'm so sorry you got dragged into this."

"What *have* I been dragged into, Jessie? I'm totally in the dark, here. Surely this can't just be about whether you can recognize people or not. Why are the police here? What's going on?"

She sighed and sat back in her chair. Jamie released his death grip on the arms of his chair. "It's a long story." She glanced around. "And this isn't the time or place to tell it. I'm sorry, Jamie. Richard and the cops made a huge point of telling me not to talk about any of this to anyone. And I don't want to involve you any more than you already are. It's...complicated." Her eyes filled, but she fought to maintain control.

He saw the stress she was under. He recognized that she needed his friendship and support now — more than he needed her to fill him in on what was happening. "It's complicated?" His tone was light, now. "Sounds like a Facebook relationship status update." He grinned.

Jessica smiled, despite herself. "Well, that's something I might be able to talk to you about. But this isn't the time or place," she said, smirking.

"Oh, really? Girl, are you saying that the dating project is seeing some progress? My, my. We've *got* to go to lunch tomorrow."

"Deal."

"And put that lei back on before it wilts. We need more color around here."

***

Tanner was in a foul mood when the detectives finally let him return to his office after hours of questioning. It had been like a fencing competition with no rules. Detective Fugate would advance, advance, advance, then lunge. Tanner would parry and attack, but his strike would aim at Jessica's credibility, not at the questioner.

He reiterated the points he had made with De Graaf, now perfecting and embellishing his act. Yes, James Rosenkrantz had come to him not only to report Jessica's brain injury but also to disclose her erratic and confused behavior. Tanner knew Jamie would deny any such meeting, so why not make as much of it as possible? Yes, Detective, Jessica was adamant about having met with Albert Covington when he was actually off at a conference.

Tanner waited carefully for the moment when the detectives would produce the list of sixty-three clients that had shaken him when De Graaf presented it. Instead of that summary sheet, however, Detective Freeman pulled a stapled bundle of papers from a folder, set them before Tanner, then sat back in her chair, silently taking notes as she had throughout the interview. Tanner slid his palm across the top of his head as he stared at the top sheet. It showed the control form for one of the large clients — and it clearly listed DOT Associates as the payee.

He assumed the remaining pages in the stack showed the control forms for the rest of the sixty-three customers. *That bitch must have gathered all this together — before Kovac cleared all the forms.* He gathered himself together, and performed an admirable scene of absolute non-recognition, asking innocently, "What am I looking at here?"

The black detective left the room. The fencing match with Fugate had resumed, but Tanner had remained steadfast, insisting that he had absolutely no clue what the printouts meant, had never heard of DOT Associates — meanwhile spewing a stream of innuendos and caring concerns about Jessica's mental stability and ability to discern reality versus fantasy. He was pleased with his performance.

His *pièce de résistance*, however, was telling the cop that Jessica had threatened to frame him when he put her on probation for hiding her medical condition which was interfering with her work and for accessing client data without authorization. Certainly that explained the coincidence that so concerned the detective — Jessica was the one who came up with D - O - T from Tanner's initials. Oh my — you don't suppose she actually opened a bank account using that name, do you Detective?

But now, back in his office at the end of an extremely long day, he paced in front of the window, fuming. His pent-up anger and tension boiled up like the towering thunderclouds building above the foothills in the distance. He snatched his phone from its holder on his belt and stabbed at the screen to place a call. Damn — it went to voicemail. Could the cops still be questioning him? "6:30. Same place." He ended the call. Maybe the kid had been arrested. He wouldn't risk calling again — he'd have to wait to see if he showed.

CHAPTER 32

Chase Kovac was already seated at the back table in the sports bar when Tanner arrived. He threw back a shot, then placed the glass next to another empty shot glass in front of him. Kovac started to signal the waitress for two more, but Tanner grabbed his arm and forced it to the table. "You need to be clear-headed for this," he snarled. "Two coffees," he said to the waitress, who had come over to get their orders. She didn't stay to ask if they wanted anything else.

"What did you tell them?"

Kovac sat back, draping an arm along the back of the empty chair beside him, trying to look cool. "Nothing, man. Told them I hardly even know who that chick is. Maybe was introduced once at a company meeting." He smirked.

"What about that program you got from that freak consultant? Did you tell them you didn't know who he was either?"

"No. I figured they wouldn't buy *two* people lying about meeting with me. Said I was taking a class on writing game software. Wanted to make my project really cool, so I asked Kozerski for help and he wrote *Superior_Random* for me. Then

— this is totally sweet — I told them that *Jess-i-ca* —" He drew out her name in a snide, derisive voice. "— came up to me after eavesdropping on Kozerski and me and asked me a bunch of questions about what I was working on." He snickered, delighted at his perceived cleverness.

"If you had admitted in the first place that the programming part was over your head, and not gone off and asked Checkers the Clown for help..."

"Hey — it's not like you've brought much to the table here, Tanner. Drop it."

The waitress dropped off two mugs of coffee and a container of sweeteners and powdered creamer. They sat silently until she had moved away.

Tanner re-focused on the present situation. "Okay. Here's where we are. The cops are looking at Stein's story versus ours — she said / he said. I've thrown out some stuff to make them doubt her side, but as long as she continues to stick with her story, things could go either way."

"They showed you the printouts of those control records, right? We can say she just made those up to cover her tracks. They're going to call up all those client accounts and look at what's there, and they're going to see blanks. She's a programmer — she could dummy up the printouts, no problem."

Tanner decided not to tell Kovac about the other seeds he had planted in the detective's mind. He preferred dealing with the kid on a "need to know" basis. "We've got to start putting pressure on her to back off from her story. Plenty of pressure, and quickly."

"Such as...?"

"Find her weak spots. We're already hitting on her honesty, her mental stability. I'm sure that's coming through to her when the cops are talking to her. But we need to be more direct.

Follow her. Find out who her friends are outside of work. Maybe we can get to her with threats against her friends."

"We've got her home address. I guarantee I can make her feel threatened." Kovac clenched his fists, already working himself up into a rage.

Tanner grimaced. "Jesus, Kovac. You don't ever learn, do you? You've gotten away with that kind of shit so far, but that won't last. You've got to control your temper and use your head. For a smart guy, you can sure be an idiot."

The kid had inherited his intelligence from his mother — the Tanner side of the family. Unfortunately, Kovac also inherited his father's volatile and violent temper. Tanner was relieved that his sister had long since dumped the guy, but not before his nephew had picked up a lot of bad and ultimately dangerous traits.

Kovac glared at him, but slowly relaxed his hands, placing them palm-down on the table.

"Okay, so I follow her. Figure out who she hangs with."

"Exactly. Feed me whatever you learn — I'll do some detective work of my own and find out more about her friends. We'll find some weaknesses and go after them. Meanwhile, let's keep her off balance. Confuse her with general threats from people she can't recognize." Tanner smirked, indicating the two of them. "We'll need some phones...."

Kovac snickered. "I'm a fucking boy scout — always prepared," he said as he pulled five cell phones out of his briefcase, spreading them on the table as if he were displaying a winning hand of poker. "Pick a phone, any phone."

"Untraceable?" Kovac nodded.

"Okay, then. Let's get this rolling tonight."

***

It was still light out when he guided his car into a parking spot at the curb of the residential area. He had a clear view of the front yard of Jessica's small house on the opposite side of the street, but figured he might draw too much attention from her next-door neighbors if he just sat in his vehicle for any length of time. Her front door was open, and he thought he could make out a figure moving within the house at times.

Two teenaged boys jogged past. He sat for a few more minutes. A woman walked by at a brisk pace, wearing bright-white sneakers and carrying a shocking pink water bottle. A couple on bikes glided past.

Kovac pulled the bill of his baseball cap a bit lower, then slid out of the car. He had changed out of his work clothes before leaving the bar downtown, so he figured he wouldn't look out of place as another person out for some exercise after work. He headed in the direction the others had gone, casually glancing back at Jessica's house until it was almost out of sight. He knelt on one knee, pretending to tie a shoe, rose, crossed the street, and headed back toward her property in a slow stroll.

As he walked along the sidewalk directly in front of Jessica's house, he pulled his hat down even further and checked that his sunglasses were in place. He turned his head away, pretending to have noticed something across the street, but then chuckled, realizing she probably couldn't recognize him even without his slight disguise. He continued his stroll, again checking over his shoulder occasionally in case she left the house.

Yes! Just as he was preparing to cross the street and double-back to his parked car, he spotted Jessica striding purposefully across her front lawn and onto the sidewalk. Her back was to Kovac as she walked briskly away. He followed, matching her pace and nearly half a block behind.

Jessica turned onto a path that took her onto the Highline Canal trail. The sun had just dipped behind the mountains, and the evening was still quite warm. The typical afternoon build-up of cumulus clouds had begun, but no thunderstorms seemed likely. Jessica moved along at a quick clip, her head down. Kovac watched her as he maintained his distance. He noted other walkers, joggers, and bicyclists using the path, checking his watch from time to time. Jessica still strode on, but the numbers of people were dropping.

The light was fading. She stopped at an intersection with a road, but this time didn't cross. She turned around, and started back the way she had come. Kovac hesitated a moment, then continued toward her. He glanced over his shoulder. All clear.

They continued to converge. Jessica had a frown on her face and was staring at the ground just in front of her as she marched, deep in thought. Kovac scanned quickly to the canal side of the path, looking for a spot that would be hidden by the huge cottonwood trunks. She would be beside him in a few more steps.

He started to shift his path to block her when a voice rang out, "Bike — on your left." He looked past her shoulder and detected a man on a bike coming up behind her and slowing, waiting for the two pedestrians to give him an opening to pass. A second bike was following close behind.

Jessica stepped to the right edge of the trail, making room for the bikes to pass. She continued walking past Kovac, who grudgingly stepped out of the middle of the path as well. Both bicyclists passed at a very slow speed, each rider glancing back several times at the walkers as they rolled away. Kovac had turned to watch Jessica and the bicyclists, but realized he was drawing attention. He spun back around and continued the way he had been going until he reached the road. Only then did he look for the riders. They were out of sight, and so was Jessica.

Kovac took his time walking back along the trail to Jessica's neighborhood and to his car. He stuck his sunglasses atop the ball cap and made careful observations of areas of vegetation along the path, sight lines where the path curved, distances from road crossings.

Just in case.

CHAPTER 33

Jessica rolled over and slapped at her alarm clock, vaguely wondering why it was so incredibly dark at six in the morning. The sound continued. She switched on the light by her bed and squinted at it — 1:47. She finally roused herself enough to realize it was her phone that was playing the theme from *Close Encounters of the Third Kind*. She grabbed it, frowning at the "Unknown" caller ID displayed, but decided to answer, concerned that it might be some sort of emergency.

"Hello?" she croaked, her voice still not ready to be awake.

"You need to back off — now!" a gruff voice muttered. "No one believes you. Keep this up, and you'll lose your job. I'll make sure no one will ever hire you again. You're just some brain-damaged schizophrenic who dreamed up a conspiracy. None of it's real. You created the whole thing in your whacked-out mind. Back off before you ruin your life."

She was totally awake now. "Who is this?" she said, trying to control the trembling of her voice.

"We're watching you. BACK OFF."

The call ended.

Jessica jettisoned the phone onto the nightstand as if it had burned her. Her heart was hammering in her chest, her breathing shallow and rapid. She felt like she was making a series of desperate rock climbing moves, knowing she would take a long fall if she failed. She began repeating a mantra silently — *Calm. Calm. Deep breaths. Calm.*

When she thought she'd be capable of speaking, she took one more deep breath and reached for the phone. The *Close Encounters* tones began again, and she jumped to her feet. "Unknown" was blazoned across the phone's display. Another sound began competing with the ringtone as her cat loudly announced his demands to be admitted to the bedroom. She let Pooka in, and he immediately jumped onto the bed and snuggled under the covers she had thrown back.

As soon as the phone stopped ringing, Jessica snatched it up. She pressed 9 and 1, then stopped. Should she call Detective Freeman — LaKeisha — directly? She had the detective's business card. She glanced at the clock. Almost two in the morning. Was this really something that had to be handled in the middle of the night? She could report it in the morning. She wouldn't be surprised if the detectives were back in DenDev's office again in the morning. Later *this* morning, she reminded herself.

Jessica checked to see if the caller had left a message the second time around. No. She tried to think if his voice had sounded familiar. Too hard to tell — he had spoken in a loud whisper, and was probably trying to disguise his voice.

The phone started up again. She turned it off, padded out to the kitchen and left it on the counter before returning to the bedroom.

She usually didn't let Pooka sleep with her, but decided she wanted his company tonight. She left the bedroom door ajar just enough so he could slip in and out as he pleased, then joined him in the bed. He began kneading her arm, purring happily. She lay awake, staring blindly at the dim shadows of the darkened room, the caller's words playing over and over in her mind.

***

Although she seldom wore makeup, Jessica decided today would be the exception. She dabbed foundation on the dark circles beneath her red eyes, hoping to lessen the raccoon look that confronted her when she looked in the bathroom mirror that morning. She had finally dozed off again after hours laying awake. Then the damn alarm clock had gone off for real.

She had considered calling in sick, but thought that would look very bad, considering. The gang was planning on climbing after work today. She thought of backing off on that as well, but realized that getting out with friends and focusing on nothing but climbing was probably *exactly* what she needed.

She dragged herself through her morning routine and plodded down the road to the light rail station, her briefcase in one hand, a small duffle in the other. She didn't notice the car that pulled out of a spot near her house once she was a half block away. It crept behind her until she crossed a busy street. The car turned and headed for the on-ramp to the Interstate highway.

"She should be on the next train. The schedule says it's due to arrive there at 7:18."

"I'll find her."

Jessica dozed as the electric train rumbled its familiar thump-thump, thump-thump along the rails. Another passenger gently shook her shoulder and she awoke with a start. Most of the passengers had already departed — they were at the downtown terminal.

She shook off her grogginess and fell into the herd of office workers streaming out of the station, heading for their various office buildings. As the crowd thinned slightly, a man rushed up behind her.

"Jessica! Jessica — is that you?" He reached out and placed a hand on her shoulder.

Jessica turned to face a man beaming at her. She had no idea who he was, but smiled tentatively back at him.

"I can't believe we ran into each other like this. It's so wonderful to see you, sweetheart!" He threw his arms around her, giving her a bear hug and kissing her noisily on the cheek.

Was this an old friend of her parents? Her uncle who lives in California? Jessica stared into his face as he held her at arms' length, gleefully looking into her face.

"It's great to see you, too," she ad-libbed. "How long's it been?" she added, hoping for clues.

Now he looked puzzled — hurt, even. "Honey, you act like you don't recognize me."

She could swear he was actually pouting. She stammered, very embarrassed and totally at a loss for words. "I'm really sorry, but...my memory for faces is really bad."

His hands dropped to his side. "Jessica," he said, shaking his head sadly. "I can't believe you don't recognize your own father."

She gasped and backed away. Spun around and ran, dodging other pedestrians as she hurried away. She could still hear the man's laughter as she fled.

CHAPTER 34

Jessica exited the elevator and raced to the relative sanctuary of her cubicle, her head lowered to avoid any eye-contact. It was like those first few days back at work after her accident when she was in terror of encountering an acquaintance and not recognizing them. Since then, she had learned to smile back at anyone glancing her way. But not today.

She sat, eyes closed, gripping the arms of her chair, her ears pounding with her rapid heartbeat. *Calm. Deep breaths.* The thumping slowed.

Ring-ring. She jerked her eyes open as her desk phone signaled an outside call.

"Hello, this is Jessica."

Silence.

"Hello?"

"Those detectives are going to want to talk to you again. When they do, you are going to BACK OFF." His voice clipped each word precisely. "They can't decide if *you're* the thief or you're just delusional. Your choice: Prison or a Shrink. Up to you."

"Who is this?" Jessica managed to keep her voice steady and strong.

"Back off. Nobody believes you. Don't make it harder on yourself." He hung up.

She held the handset and stared at it as if she might identify the caller if she could only look closely enough. Kovac? She didn't think so. Tanner? Possibly. What about the man on the street this morning? Or last night's caller? They seemed different, but...

"Hey, Jessie. Oh, sorry — you're making a call." Jamie set down his coffee in front of her for their morning ritual.

Jessica realized she was still holding the phone. She hung up, then focused on the coffee mug in front of her. She grasped the handle and took a few swallows.

"Hello? Since when do you actually *drink* coffee?" Jamie laughed until Jessica turned toward him. "Oh my, look at those eyes. Girl, you've had a rough night. Go ahead and drink all the coffee you want. I'll get another."

"Shit. Is it that obvious? I tried using makeup..." She placed her palms over her eyes, hoping their coolness would help. Her hands were trembling.

"Jessie? What's wrong? Did something happen?" He placed his hand on her shoulder.

"What if that concussion did more damage than just the face blindness? What if I imagine stuff but then think it's real? You know, like the mathematician in *A Beautiful Mind*..." She sat upright. "Jamie, were there really detectives here yesterday questioning people?"

He knelt down so he could look her directly in the eye. "Jessie, you're not crazy. The detectives are real. You've been cranking out some great design specs. And didn't you tell me they ran a ton of tests on you to make sure nothing else was wrong?"

She nodded, hesitantly.

"Okay, then. What happened? What got you so shaken up?"

She told him about the phone calls — during the night and this morning at work. The bizarre encounter with her "father."

"I was going to call Detective Freeman first thing this morning, but then that call came in and you came and... I'll call her right now." Her usual spark had returned.

Jessica rummaged in a pocket of her briefcase, pulling out several business cards. She was reaching for her cell phone when the desk phone rang. She stared at it, afraid to answer.

Jamie reached across her desk and picked up the receiver. "Jessica's desk — Oh, wait a moment, I see her now. Hang on just a moment, Detective."

Jessica let out a long breath. They waited a few more seconds before she took the phone. "This is Jessica. — Yes, I'll be right up."

"Good. Tell them about the calls and don't worry — you're not crazy!" Jamie plucked the lei he had given Jessica from the edge of a cubicle wall where someone had moved it, and carefully draped it around her computer monitor again. "Here's to a much better day." He picked up some fallen petals from the carpet and showered them onto her desk. "Go get 'em, Wonder Woman."

***

She returned to her desk two hours later. Most of her time had been with Detective Hal Fugate as Detective Freeman took notes. She had disappeared for long stretches at a time — probably to question other employees, Jessie figured. They spent most of the first hour talking about the phone calls and the man on the street.

Had she ever seen him before? She had no idea. Could she describe him?

Caucasian. Maybe 5'9" to 6' (Jessica remembered her face hitting his upper chest during the hug). In his sixties — maybe. Medium build.

Clothing — dark jacket. Dark ball cap — she didn't remember a logo.

He looked — average. Just like most people she encountered. Average.

The rest of the time was largely a rerun of previous questions. She didn't get a clear sense of whether Fugate believed her or not. She had watched for their reactions when she described the phone calls — nothing discernable.

Her desk phone rang. She stared at it, unmoving. It continued to ring, finally going to voicemail. She waited a few minutes to see if a message had been recorded. The message light came on. She watched it, as if it might reveal information. Gingerly, she picked up the receiver and punched in her code for voice messages.

"Ms. Stein, this is Captain Johnson, Denver Police. I am calling to give you some advice which I hope you'll take very seriously. The detectives on this case know you haven't been straight with them. They aren't sure if you are out-and-out lying to them, or if you are having difficulty distinguishing truth from fantasy.

"Ms. Stein, I strongly recommend that you admit your error in the stories you've been telling my detectives. If you can do that now, we can avoid charging you with making false statements to an officer of the law and falsifying evidence. We can even help you find professional care.

"I do hope you'll take this advice very seriously. You are putting yourself in a very bad situation, and we can't let it go on any longer.

"Goodbye, Ms. Stein."

She listened to the recording a second time. Then a third.

Jessica stared out the window, watching the tiny cars and people moving about on the streets far below. She shook her head slowly.

I know what I know. I'm not crazy.

She decided the only thing to do was immerse herself in a project so she wouldn't be on pins and needles all day, wouldn't spend her day staring into space, wondering what to do next. She had evidence. They would believe that. They *had* to believe that.

When her cell phone rang, Jessica strongly considered just switching it off for the rest of the day. She couldn't resist glancing at the caller ID, and was relieved to see Jamie's name on the display. "Hey, Jessie. Are we still on for lunch today? Will the detectives let you take time to eat?"

"I'm back at my desk — I think they're done with me for the day. Where are you?"

"Just out of a meeting. Meet me in the lobby?"

"You got it." She changed shoes and picked up her cell out of habit. "Nope," she muttered as she turned it off and stuck it into a pocket of her briefcase. She headed to the elevators.

CHAPTER 35

The two were still enjoying themselves as they rode the elevator back up to the 26th floor after sharing lunch. Jamie had sensed Jessica's need to keep her mind off the trouble at work and the threatening phone calls, so he entertained her with photos and stories about his Hawaii vacation with Greg, and insisted on a report of everything she and Sam had ever said to each other.

"We haven't even been on an actual date yet!" she had insisted, but that hadn't stopped him from speculating on the potential long-term future of the relationship.

Jessica stepped into her cubicle and froze. A bulky yellow-page phone directory sat in the middle of her desk, laid open. She looked closer. Someone had drawn large red circles around the two visible pages of Psychologists. A red marker — probably the one she kept in a mug on her desk — was nested in the crease between the pages.

Something else caught her eye — the lei. The loop had been cut so it could hang in a long, straight line. One end was fastened to the top shelf of the hutch over her desk. Several inches below the dangling bottom end of the lei was the blue Smurf doll she always kept at her desk. A pair of scissors was stabbed through the toy's head, pinning it to a three-ring report binder.

"Jamie!" she called, backing away from the bizarre display until her back bumped against the office window. "Jamie!"

"Oh my god. Is that supposed to be a climbing rope?" He guided her over to his desk and sat her down. Jessica was trembling. Jamie pulled a card from his shirt pocket and grabbed his phone. "Detective Fugate? There's something you need to see right away."

***

What she had hoped would be an afternoon spent actually doing some work was stolen away by more questioning as police photographed and scrutinized every inch of her workspace. By the time she was allowed to return to her work area, most of the afternoon was shot. She spent even more time with damp paper towels wiping smudges of fine powder from the arms of her chair, the desktop, her keyboard, monitor, and telephone. She'd leave the rest to the janitorial staff who cleaned each night. The lei, phone book, red pen, and scissors were gone. Her wastebasket was empty. The Smurf doll, of course, was gone.

Not again! Jessica thought as her desk phone rang — an internal call. Finally, realizing that the call *could* be coming from the detectives, she picked up.

"Jessica, please come to my office." Paula Miramonte sounded irritated.

Oh great. Now my boss is pissed off because I'm not getting any work done.

She headed to Miramonte's private office, closing the door behind her at her boss's request. She sat. Miramonte's gaze was fixed on a notepad she held in her hand. After several long moments, she laid the pad down firmly on the desk and finally met Jessica's eyes.

"Jessica, I am not privy to all the details of what is going on, and I understand that there are some topics you can't address due to the on-going investigation. However, Richard and I are in agreement that the company needs to do what we can to minimize the distractions being caused by this...situation." She picked up a pen and began tapping it lightly against her opposite hand.

"I'd like you to work from home for a while. Please coordinate with Sarah. She will transfer the files you need via email. I'm afraid we will not be able to set you up with network privileges to access files from your home computer. I'm sure you can understand..."

Jessica sat rigid. In shock. She had exposed a crime and was now being treated like a criminal. Perhaps she had misread how the authorities were reacting to the case. What did they think, that she had sabotaged her own desk? Lied about the phone calls and the man on the street? Wasn't it obvious that Tanner and/or Kovac were behind the harassment?

She ordered herself to keep it together. "I'll go speak with Sarah now," she managed in a cold voice. She resisted a strong urge to slam the office door as she left.

***

If Paula Miramonte had acted chilly, Sarah McWilliams was at absolute zero. Instead of taking notes on Jessica's information needs, she shoved a note pad in front of her without a word. Jessica stood by Sarah's desk, jotting down only the major files and other documents she'd require in order to continue on her projects.

"I'll need to look up a few more things," she said, passing her notes back to Sarah. "I can't remember them off the top of my head."

"They've taken your computer. Look them up here," Sarah said, rolling her chair back from her monitor and keyboard.

"What? Who's taken my computer? Why would they..." She bit her lip, regaining control. *This is bullshit*, she said silently.

"Fine." Jessica didn't bother looking for another chair to use. She crouched over the desk, using Sarah's computer to navigate to the additional folders she might need. She added a few more notes to her list. Sarah sat watching closely, her arms folded across her chest.

As Jessica turned to leave, Sarah spoke up.

"Next time you ask someone to stick their neck out for you, don't rat them out."

Is that what she's so ticked off about? The Client Access password?

"Sarah, I'm sorry. I didn't say anything about how I got the password until the detectives asked me directly. I couldn't lie to them about it. They were already acting like they might not believe me on..." Jessica paused, realizing that Sarah probably wasn't privy to a lot of details of what was being investigated. "...on several matters."

Sarah's cold glare remained. "*They* aren't the only ones." She rolled her chair toward the desk again, literally bumping Jessica to get her to move out of the way. "I need to get this finished. We're done here."

Jessica didn't bother responding.

When she returned to her cubicle, her computer tower was missing. Cables from the monitor and keyboard dangled empty below the desk. She sat, staring at the duffle she had brought to work with her climbing gear, considering going directly home and getting some badly-needed sleep to make up for last night.

No, going climbing is probably the best thing I could do for my sanity.

She noted that she'd need to leave in another twenty-five minutes to catch the bus to meet Marilyn and Jordan at the Park-and-Ride. She busied herself in the meantime with straightening out her desk and removing a few photos from the walls of her cubicle. She was beginning to wonder how long her exile might last. Or if she would *want* to return.

She hoped to say goodbye to Jamie before taking off, but he was nowhere to be seen. Based on several other empty cubicles she passed on her way out, she assumed they were all in a meeting, trying to make up for all the lost time of recent days.

CHAPTER 36

"Got her. You were right — she's not heading home. She's on an express bus that goes to the Federal Center. Try that first."

"I'm on it. I'll let you know if I miss her. Otherwise, you're good to go."

Tanner took his time walking back to his car in a parking garage. He commended himself for his composure when the detectives called him back in for questioning again this afternoon. Then again, he had rehearsed the scene in his mind quite carefully.

He had sensed that the cops weren't buying his theories that pinned everything on the girl. Fine. They already had several strong leads pointing at Kovac. When they shoved a photo of the Smurf Murder Scene (as he fondly thought of it) in front of him, he reacted with shock. Very convincing, he thought.

Where was he during lunch?

That was the ringer. He pulled a current printout of Chase Kovac's (a.k.a. Kevin Chase, a.k.a. Karl Chase) criminal background report from his briefcase — the *real* background report. "I was just about to bring this to you, Detective. I overheard Mr. Kovac — or whatever his name really is — making a call and referring to himself as Kevin Chase."

Just to make sure he had not only thrown Kovac under the bus, but left him there to rot, Tanner had thrown out a few zingers about his volatile and sometimes violent behavior.

***

Marilyn and Jordan greeted her as Jessica stepped off the bus. Jordan gave her a hug first. Instead of hugging her, Marilyn held her by the shoulders — much as the man who accosted her on the street had done this morning — and declared, "You look like shit. What's going on, Sista?"

Leave it to Marilyn to get right to the point. Jessica didn't want to start telling her friend about all the insanity that had happened since they had talked about going to De Graaf with her findings. She didn't even want to *think* about it tonight.

"I just didn't get much sleep last night. Somebody's dog was barking. And it's been kind of crazy at work."

"Speaking of which — what's going on with *CSI: DenDev*? You haven't said much about that since you went and talked to the big boss."

"Oh, nothing much to tell. The detectives are doing their thing — thanks to all our sticky notes on your table, of course — and I'm just trying to focus on my work while they figure it all out. Who else is coming climbing tonight?" she added, hoping to change the subject.

"I'm not sure. Sam, of course," Marilyn nudged her with a hip as they walked to Jordan's car, "and Allison said she might be there. Other than that, no idea."

Jessica tossed her duffle and briefcase into the back of the car. A few minutes later, Sam drove up and joined them, adding additional gear to the back. "Hey, I'll drive next time," he said as Marilyn and Jordan slipped into the front seats. He smiled that radiant smile of his, and greeted Jessica with a hug. They stepped back ever so slightly, smiling at each other, their arms still partially entwined.

"Yo! Are you two going climbing with us, or should we just leave you here?" Marilyn said, leaning out the passenger window.

They broke their embrace and climbed into the back seat. "Climb on!" Sam declared as he reached to hold Jessica's hand.

None of them noticed the car circling slowly through the parking lot. They didn't observe it following them as they drove to Golden.

***

After dragging herself up the steep trail, Jessica simply sat and watched the others take a turn climbing. She eventually wriggled into her harness and offered to belay Sam on his second climb of the evening. He encouraged her to take a shot on an easy route, but she barely had the energy to make it to the top. She offered to be the "belay slave" for anyone who wanted to climb, but her friends declined, suggesting that she just relax, maybe even take a nap.

Jessica found a spot to sit where she could observe several climbs at once, and settled in. The others checked in with her between climbs, but soon recognized that she was content with watching and not very interested in chatting. She paid particular attention to Sam, who was easy to pick out with his green helmet. Most of the other climbers wore white, silver, or gray.

Marilyn had disappeared for several minutes, but now returned to the area where they were climbing, laughing and calling out for everyone to hear a story.

"So there I was, taking a pee, enjoying the view and aroma of the beer factory, when I saw this photographer down there," she pointed to an area below where they had been climbing. "He's going to get home and look for that perfect 'hero shot' of all you stud climbers," she said, waving an arm to indicate everyone listening, "and he's going to find a perfect 'moon shot' instead." She leaned over, sticking her butt out behind her and wiggling it, much to the delight of her audience.

Jessica laughed along with the rest, delighted at her friend's antics. Then she stopped cold. She jumped to her feet and scanned the hillside below, looking for the photographer. She spotted someone picking his way across the slope, possibly heading toward the parking lot, which was out of view from her angle. He had a baseball cap on backwards, and was wearing a light-colored t-shirt and jeans. He stopped, faced uphill, and aimed a camera with a large lens in her general direction. A moment later he jerked the camera away from his face, spun his ball cap around so the bill shaded his face, ducked his head, and hurried toward the parking lot.

"Shit," Jessica whispered. She hesitated, wondering if she should tell anyone of her concerns. Or would they think she was nuts, freaking out over some photographer taking pictures of people climbing? Maybe it was nothing. Why would Kovac or Tanner be interested in taking pictures of her, anyway? Or, the police...?

She shook away the thoughts. *Just because I'm paranoid doesn't mean they're not out to get me!* She settled back into her spot, and tried to focus on watching her friends climb.

As they drove back to the Park and Ride to drop off Sam, Jessica's exhaustion had caught up with her. She dozed in the car, waking briefly to bid Sam goodbye, then slept until Jordan pulled up in front of her house. "Rest up, Jess. Take a nice warm bath and get to bed early. Call me if you want to talk about anything."

"I know, Mar. Sorry I was such a lump tonight. I'll talk to you soon. G'night, Jordan. Thanks for the ride." She retrieved her belongings and shuffled to the garage door. She punched in the code on the wireless garage door keypad and headed inside, ready to crash.

After feeding Pooka, she heard a flapping sound from the front of the house. The wind had kicked up with an evening thunderstorm building over the eastern plains. She flipped on the porch light and opened the door. A flyer of some sort had been stuffed partway into the locked storm door and was waving wildly in the wind. She was able to pinch one corner as she opened the door to retrieve it. Probably an ad. She tossed it onto the living room floor, then re-locked the door and flipped off the light.

The cat, of course, decided the flyer was an ideal object to attack. Then sit on. She let him enjoy his new toy while she washed up for bed. Figuring the crinkling sounds he was producing with the paper (not to mention his vocalizations and surprisingly-loud galloping noises as he attacked it from behind the couch) would disrupt her sleep, she decided to end his frolicking for the night.

She picked up the crinkled flyer and stared at the message written on it.

"BACK OFF NOW! We're done playing games."

***

Kovac was pleased with his reconnaissance job. Armed with license plate numbers and car models photographed in the Park and Ride, numerous pictures of Jordan, Sam, and Marilyn from the parking lot as well as while climbing, Tanner had assured him they'd soon know full names, employers, and home addresses of the people Jessica had spent time with all evening.

Things had gone even better than he expected. After Jessica and her friends hiked down from the cliff base, he headed up top. Scrambled up to the top of the formation for a look around. Chatted with a couple of younger guys, acting like he was new to climbing and wanted to check it out. Asked a bunch of questions. Learned a few names.

He drove home, planning to download photos from his digital SLR camera and send the best ones to Tanner. As he turned onto his block, something caught his eye. He was a car fanatic, always noticing models and makes. He knew the vehicles his neighbors drove. But he didn't know the dark sedan parked across from his house. He drove past his driveway, not changing speed. Checked out the mystery car in his mirror. Something didn't feel right.

He drove to the end of the block and turned, heading for the local supermarket. A modest number of customers still roamed the aisles at this hour. He took his time, picking up a few items so he wouldn't seem out of place. A half hour later, he circled back to his block, driving the opposite direction down the street this time. The vehicle was still there, and this time his headlights helped him confirm that at least one person was in it. He drove on.

Hours later, in a motel room across town, he lay sprawled on the bed, a near-empty bottle of tequila in one hand. "Fuckin' bitch. We warned her. Enough of this bullshit. She'll back off after I'm done with her."

He flung the bottle across the room, barely missing the old, bulky TV. It crashed against the wall, shattering. "Hey, keep it down!" someone shouted from the next room.

He found that hilarious.

CHAPTER 37

After the second night in a row of little or no sleep, Jessica was a zombie. Her call to Detective LaKeisha Freeman the previous night had led to a late session with police visiting her home to retrieve the flyer and canvas neighbors about any unusual activity they may have witnessed. Things settled down around ten p.m., but despite assurances that the cops would patrol her neighborhood more frequently starting that night, Jessica still couldn't shut off the agitated movie in her head, replaying scene after scene.

She dragged herself out of bed at eight o'clock — hours after her normal wake-up time for a work day. She nearly fell asleep again while standing under the bliss of a hot shower. Her routine was shaken; she was at a loss for what to do on a work day that wasn't like any other work day.

She turned on her cell phone to check for messages, and couldn't resist looking at the list of missed calls. A cascade of "Unknown" callers appeared, many with the same phone number. The police had already checked the number out — it was bogus. They were continuing to trace the origin of the calls.

Another couple of numbers had shown up in the past twenty-four hours. She'd need to report those to the detectives as well.

One good thing about working at home: all incoming calls would have some sort of caller ID. She wouldn't answer if she didn't recognize the caller.

As if she had caused it to happen by turning on her phone, it rang. She was relieved to see who was calling.

"Hello, LaKeisha."

They talked for several minutes. No, there hadn't been any other incidents overnight. Yes, she planned to be home all day, other than possibly running to the grocery store. She passed along the additional "unknown" phone numbers and agreed to keep her phone turned on so the detective could reach her easily.

She settled in front of her computer and downloaded the files Sarah had sent over. The sounds of traffic drifted in through the open window in her spare bedroom office. Birds sang. She wasn't accustomed to hearing outdoor sounds while working. The windows of the skyscraper where DenDev was housed didn't open.

Just as she finally focused in on a task to work on, the doorbell rang. Usually she relied on the locked storm door for security when she was home, its window panes replaced by screens to let in the breeze. Not today. Despite the pleasant morning temperature, she had kept her front door closed and locked.

She looked through the peek-hole. A gray-haired woman stood on the porch, a plate in one hand. The other was fiddling with something as Jessica heard the storm door unlock. She smiled, and opened the wooden door as well.

"Jessie — I didn't think you'd be home, but I didn't want to startle you if you were." Her neighbor, Della, stepped inside. "The police stopped by last night asking if we'd seen anyone near your house, and I was worried about you, so I baked some chocolate walnut cookies —" She had already made her way to the kitchen, and deposited the plate of cookies on the counter. Pooka was dancing around her ankles in joy. "— and something special for my little friend." As usual, she unwrapped a special nugget of some leftover prey — deliciously prepared, of course — and delivered it to the cat's bowl where he devoured it noisily.

"I guess I don't need to leave you the note now," she said. "Did someone break in? We were so worried about you, Jessie. Why were the police here?" She had flung her arms around Jessica, and was holding her tight as if she could protect her from anything and everything.

Jessica hugged her back, then extracted herself. "It's nothing that serious, Della. Thank you so much for watching out for me, though. And thanks for bringing over my favorite cookies."

Della was not to be distracted. "What *did* happen? Why were the police asking about strangers coming to your house?"

Jessica fumbled for an answer that wouldn't alarm her neighbor too much. "We've had some problems at work where they think someone is trying to steal...company secrets." *Good one, Jess.* "Another neighbor thought they saw a stranger hanging around my house, so they called the police. We figure he might be trying to break in to see if I have any company files here..." *Oops, dial it back. That might alarm her.* "But we decided he was just trying to talk to me to see if I'd slip up and tell him something about...the secrets." *I'm digging myself into a hole. Stop now.*

Della furrowed her brow, trying to make sense of Jessica's extemporaneous explanation. After a moment her face relaxed. She had either given up or chosen to simply accept it and move on.

"Meanwhile, they've got me working from home for a bit, so I guess I'd better get back on the job. Thanks again for the cookies, Della, and please don't you and Frank worry. The police are taking care of everything." *I hope*, she added silently.

After another motherly hug, Della departed and Jessica returned to her desk, battling the reruns in her head until she finally lost herself in her work.

***

Kovac nodded as he read the private message sent to him on an online climbing forum. He had just set up a user account an hour earlier, and posted his first message in a Denver-Area Climbing section.

"Got good photos of climbers at North Table mountain yesterday - would like to share with them. If you recognize the climbers in this photo, send me a private message."

He attached a photo he had taken where Marilyn, Jordan, and Sam could be seen. Jordan was belaying as Marilyn climbed. Sam was belaying a climb close by, but he had cropped the photo so Jessica was out of the picture.

Someone going by the user name *ItWasntMe* had just replied. "That's Marilyn Morrison and Jordan on the left — don't remember his last name. Sam is the guy with the green helmet, belaying. I can get in touch with Marilyn and have her send you her email address."

He fired off a response. "Do you know if she'll be climbing at North Table again soon? I've made a couple of large prints of 2 shots that came out really good & would like to give those to her & friends in person."

He waited, noting that the person he was corresponding with was still online. Less than a minute later another note popped up. "Cool. We're going out there again this Saturday. Hope to meet you then."

Kovac pumped a fist in the air.

***

The two men huddled over a web of notes and photographs spread out on a dingy bedspread in a dingier motel room. Tanner was a pro at what some called *social engineering*. Ask the right questions, act like you know more than you do, touch on peoples' desire to be helpful, and get them to divulge information that they wouldn't give out directly. Kovac had a knack for skilled gab as well — when his temper didn't get in the way. It was safer to have him work through online sources.

They were building a social network of sorts, with Jessica at the core of their web. Learn where she would be and when, who she might be with, when she'd likely be alone.

Kovac had created a diagram of names he had gleaned from Jessica's online activity. Facebook friends, friends of friends — focusing on people she seemed to know through climbing. He followed up on their leads using emails, posts, and private messages, while Tanner made phone calls.

"Hi, Tom? I'm hoping you can help me out. You climb with Sam Kellerman, right? — I have a jacket he left in my car, and I can't get a hold of him. Do you know if he'll be climbing with the gang at North Table on Saturday? I can bring it to him there." — "Oh, you guys are training for Mt. Rainier this weekend? Well, I'll just try to reach him next week then."

Their web grew.

***

Jessica stood, stretching her stiff back. Other than a short break for a light lunch of leftovers from the fridge, and a trip or two to the bathroom, she had barely moved from her spot in front of the computer all day. She was shocked to realize it was already six thirty in the evening.

The "unknown" caller seemed to have given up on that tactic. She had received several text messages during the day, but no voice calls. Jamie texted that he missed her at work, and wanted to know if she needed him to stop by each morning with coffee for her to smell. Both Marilyn and Sam had asked if she was feeling better today. She had sent off light-hearted responses to each of them, then dove back into her work.

She didn't feel like cooking, even though she usually got a lot of enjoyment out of it. She plucked a frozen entrée from the freezer and stuck it in the microwave. She ate her heated meal without tasting it — perhaps not such a bad thing — and occupied herself with a rousing game with the cat involving an empty shoe and a wad of aluminum foil. She tried watching a movie, but became frustrated with the two — three? four? — thirty-something male characters who all looked the same to her.

I need to get out. Go for a walk.

That always helped her mood. The sun was low in the west, shaded by some clouds over the mountains. The temperature was still quite warm, but not unpleasant. She slipped on her favorite sneakers, checked that her doors were all locked, and exited through the garage so she wouldn't need a key to get back in.

Jessica headed for the Highline Canal trail access near her home — familiar turf. She realized after setting off on the path that she had left her phone sitting by her computer at home. *The hell with it,* she thought. *I'll be back in a half hour, forty-five minutes. Detective Freeman can just wait for me to call her back if she needs to talk to me.*

She lost herself in the sounds and smells that surrounded her as she enjoyed her little escape from the stress of recent weeks. She managed to tune out the sounds of vehicles which were muffled by the dense vegetation anyway. Birds were announcing the approaching dusk and a squirrel scolded her from its perch on the trunk of a cottonwood. Her thoughts turned to tomorrow's dinner date with Sam, and she strode along with a bounce in her step.

She heard a rustling and was shocked as a strong hand grabbed her arm from behind. She began to shout, but another hand wrapped over her mouth, smothering most of the sound. She struggled wildly, trying to free her arms which her attacker had now pinned with a diaphragm-crushing hug. She tried to stomp on the arch of his foot, or kick backward into his knee, but she only dealt glancing blows. As he started to drag her toward the trees and bushes, she managed to free one arm. She clawed desperately over her shoulder at his face, trying to find his eyes. His glasses protected him from her fingers long enough for him to curb her efforts by throwing her to the ground. She felt a sharp pain in her cheek and abdomen as she landed face-first on the exposed roots of an ancient tree. Although she was gasping for breath, she managed an abbreviated scream.

The man flipped her onto her back and pounced upon her. One hand again covered her mouth. Her legs were pinned to the ground as he straddled her thighs. His oversized sunglasses were askew, but still hid his eyes and upper cheeks. A hoodie cinched tight around his face hid his forehead, hair, and ears.

"Fuckin' bitch. Maybe you'll listen to *this*." He jerked her head violently to one side, still covering her mouth, then reached for the button fastening her shorts with the other.

"Hey! What's going on! Hey!" A man's voice called out. Jessica could hear footsteps pounding, running. "Leave her alone!" a woman's voice shouted. More pounding footsteps, drawing closer.

The man sprung to his feet, took a few steps, and grabbed a bicycle which Jessica noticed for the first time. He jumped onto it at a run, racing away from the voices and the footsteps.

An instant later, a man ran past in pursuit of the man in the hoodie. A woman dropped to her knees beside Jessica, panting heavily. "Are you hurt?" she gasped.

Jessica couldn't gather her thoughts enough to know if she was hurt. She could only feel her heaving chest as she tried to remember what it was like to breath normally. She managed to nod at the woman, unable to speak. Afraid that she would start to scream if she tried to make any sound at all. Afraid that she wouldn't be able to stop screaming.

The woman looked over her shoulder as her companion returned, hands on his hips, his chest heaving. He shook his head. He hadn't been able to run fast enough to catch the attacker on the bike.

"I'm Pat. This is my husband, Michael. We're going to stay here with you until the police get here." She handed Michael a cell phone to call 9-1-1. Pat crouched beside Jessica on the ground, her hand resting gently on her shoulder. "It's going to be all right. We're right here."

Jessica's breathing began to settle down. She could still feel her heart pounding, but the rate was gradually slowing. "Thank you," she whispered. Pat squeezed her shoulder.

Within a few minutes, Michael spotted two uniformed police officers rushing along the path toward them and waved his arms. By this time, Jessica was sitting up, Pat still close by. The female officer knelt down beside the two women, introducing herself as Sharon Garcia.

Officer Garcia had Pat go talk to her partner, Officer Daniel Trimble. She questioned Jessica with a calm voice. Was she injured? Had she been sexually assaulted? Jessica answered the questions in a monotonic voice, feeling as if she were watching the entire scene from a distance. Or in a dream.

Additional officers arrived — some in uniform, others not. Officer Garcia excused herself for a minute and conferred with others out of Jessica's hearing range. A man in dark slacks and a light-colored shirt stepped away from the group and approached Jessica. Totally bald, mustache. She snapped out of her daze. "Detective Fugate — I'm glad you're here. Is LaKeisha, um, Detective Freeman here, too?" She looked around anxiously for a black female with very short hair.

The officer looked at her oddly. "Sorry, ma'am, I'm not Detective Fugate. I'm here to collect evidence." He was studying the area around her as he spoke. "Fingernail clippings for now. We can collect any clothing that might contain evidence once we get you back to your house." He shone a bright light on the ground beside her. "We'll be working around this area for a little while. I understand you may have scratched the perp's face?"

She nodded.

"Good. Let's take care of the fingernails now. Then I believe Officers Garcia and Trimble will drive you home, and I'll meet with you again shortly." He helped her to her feet and carefully took samples of whatever was under her fingernails, then trimmed her nails very short, collecting everything in containers which he labeled.

Before Officer Garcia escorted her to the patrol car waiting at the nearest intersection with the trail, Jessica asked for a moment with her rescuers. She hugged Pat and Michael, thanking them again for chasing away her attacker.

Back in her own home, more questioning ensued. Police officials came and went. They asked again if she needed medical attention, and again she declined. She had scrapes on her knees and elbows, her cheek was slightly swollen and quite tender, and her abs ached, but she didn't feel like anything was broken or needed more than a bit of cleaning with soap and water. Physically, this was nothing compared to falling off the end of a rope. Emotionally...that remained to be seen.

Someone — Jessica assumed he was the bald officer who took the fingernail samples — stopped by to collect her leaves-and-grass-covered shirt. Detectives Freeman and Fugate arrived, conferring with the first responders who then headed out to resume their patrol of the neighborhood.

Naturally, Jessica hadn't been able to identify her attacker positively, despite having looked him straight in the face as he pinned her to the ground. The police had tried to get her to provide some sort of description of the portion of his face that was exposed, but to no avail. Pat and Michael had never gotten close enough to him to get a decent look at his face, so all the police had learned was a description of his clothing and a few vague impressions about the bicycle he used to escape.

Detective Freeman sat on the couch next to Jessica while Fugate went to the kitchen to make a few calls. Everyone else had finally cleared out.

"I understand that you can't describe your attacker's face, Jessica. But can you identify him in some other way?"

It was a relief to talk to someone who knew about her prosopagnosia, and didn't just assume she was too freaked out to remember anything. Still, Jessica had to shake her head. She was learning to rely on a variety of ways to recognize people — their voices, gestures and the way they walked, how they dressed, hair style — but there was nothing in her mind's database to help her recognize a man she had only seen hovering over her, growling angry threats.

"I think I know who it might have been, but it's just my gut feeling. I can't say that I could actually *identify* him."

"What's your gut telling you?" LaKeisha set her mouth in a tight line.

"Chase Kovac. The only real impression I got from his appearance was that the guy was fairly young — twenties, maybe thirties. But the way he said 'maybe you'll listen to this'... it seemed like he knew me. Like he was the one who's been calling or leaving messages."

LaKeisha nodded. "Jessica, we can take you to a safe house tonight. You'll be able to stay there for several days, and then we can re-evaluate the situation."

"So, you believe me!"

The detective was puzzled. "Of course I do. Obviously you were attacked. With all the threats you've received, we have to consider that the attack could be related."

"I mean, you believe that I've been telling you the truth about the money-skimming and my meetings with Tanner and Kovac and all that?"

"Of course. The evidence has all been there. Someone tried to wipe out the data, but they didn't know about your log files. And we've pinpointed when they tried to clear the data based on back-ups of client systems. Why would you think we didn't believe you?"

Jessica almost collapsed in relief. "I guess all those calls just got to me." She paused, considering something. "Do you work for Police Captain Johnson?"

"Never heard of him. Why do you ask?"

She nodded, grimly. "I guess that's one more phone call I need to report to you. It's still stored on my voice mail at work. You'll have to get someone there to retrieve it for you."

Detective Freeman jotted a note. "Well, let's get you set up with the safe house. You can pack a change of clothes, if you like. They'll be able to supply toiletries like toothpaste —"

"Must I? Can't I stay here? I have friends who can stay with me. In fact, they should be here any minute. I called them just before you got here." Her agitation had returned. Much as she worried about what Kovac might do, she still drew comfort from her familiar surroundings — her nest. From having her friends with her and having Pooka close by. She couldn't imagine having to be cooped up in an unknown place with strangers, all of them likely in dire circumstances. It sounded like hell to her.

The detective sighed. "We aren't going to force you to go anywhere. But we want you to be safe." Jessica shook her head, her eyes pleading. LaKeisha considered for a moment. "Okay. Here's what we'll do tonight. We'll put a watch on your house as well as keep up the enhanced patrol. But I don't want you here alone."

Jessie slumped back in the couch in relief. "Thank you. I feel much better about that."

"Jessica, I wish I could tell you that we're about to make an arrest in this case, but the problem is we don't have enough solid evidence yet. This person — or persons — has been pretty careful up until now. We didn't find fingerprints other than yours on the scissors and red pen or on the notes you've shown us. The calls are coming from illegally-modified phones. However, some other leads are starting to pan out. It'll take some time for DNA tests from tonight to come in, but perhaps that will add to the case. So, in the meantime, we'll do all we can to keep you safe."

The doorbell rang. Marilyn and Jordan raced through the front door before anyone could move to open it. Jessica flew to her best friend's arms, holding on to her as if she were drowning. Jordan stood close to the pair, silently rubbing Jessica's back.

The detectives offered up the safe house option one last time before advising the group of all the situations that should prompt an immediate phone call to 9-1-1. Dispatch would notify them if anything arose involving Jessica and her friends. They departed.

Marilyn and Jordan stayed up with Jessie, letting her talk out her story. They both rubbed her back and tried to comfort her when she would tremble with emotion. Finally, spent, she eased her sore body into bed. Marilyn tucked her in like a child. Pooka, who had spent hours hiding from all the unfamiliar people, established himself under one of her arms, tucked snuggly against her side.

Jordan and Marilyn snuggled close together in the guest bed, the doors to both bedrooms left open so they could hear Jessica during the night if she should need them.

CHAPTER 38

Oakley Tanner idly rearranged the three cell phones on his kitchen table, shuffling them around like a shell game. He reflected on the call from Kovac. The kid wanted the rest of his share of the money. Now.

He was disappointed with how quickly the plan had broken down. Last time they had kept it as an inside job. He had set a goal, reached it, and shut it down without anyone ever suspecting a thing. Tanner smiled, remembering the glowing letter of recommendation his former boss had written for him after he resigned so he could "move closer to family." The idiot hadn't a clue that Tanner had walked away with almost one hundred grand of company funds. Kovac — going by Kevin Chase at the time — had served him well as an assistant bookkeeper for that gig, and had been well rewarded.

His target had been a million for this round. Don't touch internal company funds. Go after a lot of much wealthier customers instead, picking up modest amounts from each one. Damn.

Now Kovac/Chase wanted the rest of his share. Tanner had added a few extra layers of laundering to the funds, and had just moved the balance to an offshore account. The initial DOT Associates accounts were closed. Chase didn't deserve a penny more.

Would Chase follow up on his threats? Could he?

Tanner shook his head. He had witnessed Chase's temper, knew he could become violent. The kid was a good thirty years younger. Strong, athletic. Tanner was a bit taller, weighed more, but — he contemplated his gut overflowing the waist of his slacks — not the right kind of extra weight. Could Chase do him serious harm? Unfortunately, the answer was yes.

It was time to make another career move — a long-distance move. He wouldn't try to finagle a good reference letter this time. He swept the cell phones into the kitchen trash bag, tied it up, and tossed it into the trunk of his car. There was a sizeable apartment complex with large trash dumpsters on his way to the airport.

CHAPTER 39

"I'm not going to spend the whole day cooped up in here, jumping out of my skin every time I hear a sound. I'm going to live my life." Jessica was pacing the living room, showing an energy level that was almost obscene for this early an hour.

"Jess, we want to know you're safe. Maybe I'll take the day off from work —"

"— and I'll do the same," Jordan said.

"No. Absolutely not." Jessica stopped pacing for a moment and planted herself in front of them, arms akimbo. "Look, I'm not going to do anything stupid. I'll tell Detective Freeman where I'm going and they'll probably send along my new friends to keep me company." She waved toward the street where an unmarked police car had been parked since late last night.

Marilyn and Jordan looked at each other, finally nodding. He shrugged. "Keep us in the loop, okay? Let us know where you are and how you're doing."

Marilyn added, "Don't hesitate to ask either of us to come meet you. We can stay again tonight."

"Actually, I have a dinner date tonight," Jessica said, grinning for the first time this morning.

"You're still going? You're not going to reschedule?" Marilyn was incredulous.

"I need to live my life. I'll work something out. Maybe it'll have to be a double-date with Detectives Freeman and Fugate — I don't know. But I'm not going to curl up here in the fetal position and wait for all this to be over." She glanced at the kitchen clock. "You guys are going to be late for work. I'll keep in touch, I promise."

She hugged both of them, thanking them again for staying with her, then escorted them to the door.

As she watched them drive away, she fetched her phone and called LaKeisha to work out the logistics of spending time at the library and the local recreation center. She didn't feel up to working out, but they had a large hot tub that sounded very appealing for her aching body.

***

Jessica stared at her image in the mirror. Her cheek had turned a nasty shade of dark purple, and she had a black eye to match. At least the bruising on her abdomen would be covered up during dinner, and if she wore her blouse with three-quarter sleeves, the scrapes on her arms would barely show.

She considered whether to call Sam and tell him about last night, or just to wait until he arrived to pick her up. It would be impossible for him *not* to notice, but perhaps seeing her up close when he heard the story rather than letting him imagine her being in far worse shape was the better plan.

Forget the makeup. It is what it is.

She selected a silky pair of light tan slacks to go with the colorful blouse — the one with the three-quarter sleeves — and added a pair of dangling earrings. She clipped her long hair up, then remembered that the style emphasized her high cheekbones. Black and blue cheekbones. Not good. She'd wear her hair down and loose.

The doorbell sounded, and her face lit up. She bounded to the door and flung it open. Sam's smile faded instantly.

"What happened? Did you do that climbing?" He stared in shock, letting his hand holding a bouquet of miniature red roses drop to his side, momentarily forgotten.

"No, but let's not talk about that right now. I'll tell you about it at dinner. Oh, those flowers are beautiful!" Distract now, talk later.

Sam was confused for a moment, then recovered. "I hope you like roses." The magic smile returned as he presented the flowers.

Jessica quickly found a vase and displayed the roses in the middle of the dining room table. "I'm ready if you are," she chirped.

They arrived at an upscale Italian restaurant in an old neighborhood east of downtown Denver. The lights were dim (much to Jessica's relief — she had worried about frightening small children with her looks). The service was smooth and, best of all, Sam was sitting beside her. They ordered wine, and Sam raised a toast "To the Future!" Clink. Jessica countered with "Back to the Future!" Clink. Sam paused, then offered a toast to "The Hobbit: There and Back Again." Clink.

He stopped her before she could think of another title. "So... how'd you get those bruises?" His hand brushed her swollen face like a gentle whisper.

She swallowed. "First of all, as you can see I'm all right." He raised his eyebrows, now more concerned than before. "I was attacked last night."

"What!" His mouth gaped open and he reached to hold her hand.

"Some runners saw this guy grab me, and they scared him off. I'm just banged up a bit, nothing major. I'm all right — really!" She met his astonished look, and fought to stay cool, not break down.

"Oh my god, Jessie. You called the police, right?" She nodded, willing herself to breathe deeply and slowly. "Have they caught him?"

"Not yet. But they're pretty sure they know who he is, and they're looking for him. Meanwhile, the police are watching over me. I feel like I'm in a cop movie." She saw Sam's expression becoming more and more concerned. "Oh, but don't worry. They decided we could go out to dinner and they wouldn't need to follow us here."

"Right. That's, uh, encouraging."

"But enough about me," she quipped. "Tell me how *your* day's been going." She pasted a smile on her lips.

He snorted, shook his head. "Okay. If that's how you want to play it. My day started out pretty ordinary, but I can't say that any longer. Jessie, I'll bet nobody's ever thought you were boring. Ah, here's our salad."

They each took a few bites before Sam paused, his fork in midair. "Wait a second. *Why* are the cops watching over you? Not that I don't think it's a good idea, but isn't that kind of unusual? Unless...they think it wasn't a random crime. That you were targeted." A horrified look came across his face. "Jessie? Was it someone you know?"

"They're not sure. *I'm* not sure. But it's possible. Listen, Sam, there's a bunch of crazy stuff going on at work that I'm not supposed to talk about while the police are doing their investigation. I'm sorry." She tried to smile. "I'd really like to put it out of my head for tonight and just enjoy our evening."

He set down his fork and reached out to give her arm a comforting squeeze. She winced in pain. "Oh no, I'm sorry." He sat back and looked her over appraisingly. "Okay. No more cross-examination. It's great to be here with you." He smiled reassuringly, and gently reached for her hand.

They returned their focus to enjoying an excellent meal and learning more about each other, avoiding the topics of police bodyguards and violent crime.

They had already figured out they both loved movies (especially oldies) and classic television shows. Climbing, of course. Jessica had earned a Masters degree in Computer Science at the University of Colorado in Boulder. She had started climbing during Grad school, but had let that slip away during the year and a half after she got her degree. Her father had battled prostate cancer during that time, and finally succumbed. She took it up again a year later and met Marilyn about that time.

Sam grew up in Oregon, and his parents and older brother still lived there. His degrees were in electrical engineering, which meant he had taken a lot of computer science classes as well. He started rock climbing as an undergrad, but also got into hiking and then mountaineering in recent years.

They both loved sixties folk music. "Maybe we were born at the wrong time," Jessica suggested. "We should have been baby-boomers."

"In my parents' case, I figure we just swapped generations. They're into hip hop, if you can believe it. They hated the Beatles, Bob Dylan. My mother has an earring in her nose. No kidding! I think we must have passed each other coming and going in some sort of time warp."

"You have an earring." Jessica affectionately caressed his earlobe. "I like it. Understated. Sexy."

"I like that you like it," he said, "and speaking of sexy, that thing you're doing with my ear..."

They became enthralled with gazing into each other's eyes. "Would you care for any dessert, tonight?" the waiter interrupted. "Our specialty is homemade tiramisu: lady fingers soaked in coffee liqueur, layered with cream and mascarpone, and finished with a dusting of Dutch cocoa, atop a swirl of dark Belgian chocolate sauce."

Their eyes widened, their faces lit up with glee. Both nodded.

"Yes, we'll have an order of tiramisu. Two forks," Sam said, his eyes not leaving Jessica's.

A dessert that looked too beautiful for words was soon delivered to their table. They picked up their forks, and each took a first sample, their gestures a perfect mirror.

"This works out so smoothly with you right-handed and me a lefty," Jessica observed.

They made a game of mirroring their movements as they enjoyed a second bite.

"Back off from the tiramisu and no one will get hurt," he said as he slid the plate away from her.

"Back off... " Jessica's smile faded when she heard the familiar phrase.

"You're right. That's not quite it. Back *away*?" he pondered. "I know — *step away* from the tiramisu and no one will get hurt." He took a bite in triumph, then slid the plate back to her. She relaxed.

Jessica giggled, and slowly dipped her finger into the cake, scooping off a creamy selection of mascarpone, drizzled chocolate, and whipped cream. She moved her finger to her mouth, removing it in slow motion, her eyes fixed on Sam's. "You forgot to be my mirror image," she noted in a husky voice, after licking her lips with just the very tip of her tongue.

"Whoa. Is it hot in here, or is it just me?" he answered. "Okay, two can play at this game." He repeated the act, bringing his tiramisu-covered finger just to his lips, then stopped, a devilish smile on his lips. He reached slowly toward her mouth with the tasty offering, a smiling question on his face.

Now she was feeling the heat. Her eyes dashed quickly from side to side, scanning to see if anyone was watching. His finger was almost to her lips. She laughed, a throaty sound, and parted her lips to accept his sensuous offering. She leaned forward slightly, taking his finger into her mouth, then closed her lips around it as he pulled out as slowly as he could.

"That's the best tiramisu I've ever tasted," she said.

Sam glanced up and over her shoulder, and burst out laughing. Their waiter was trying to look busy wiping a corner of a nearby table, but had been working on the same spot for some time. He glanced over his shoulder at the couple, likely checking to see if it was safe to approach their table. Sam hoped he had averted his eyes soon enough so that the waiter hadn't been embarrassed further.

They finished their dessert in a more traditional style — using forks — and sat holding hands as the waiter returned to drop off the check. He avoided eye contact — not that the two of them would have noticed.

They had lingered over dinner for hours and it was getting late, so they decided to head back to Jessica's house. They walked arm in arm from the restaurant to Sam's car, parked just around the corner. A leafy tree cast gentle shadows from the streetlight. They turned to each other. Sam leaned over and Jessie met his lips with hers. His hand swept through her loose, straight hair as they kissed, his other hand at her waist. She slipped her arms around him, wrapping herself close. The sensation was even more delicious than the decadent tiramisu.

With a wistful sigh, they moved apart, and climbed into the car.

When they pulled into her driveway, Jessica looked out the car window. "My Dragnet buddies are here."

"Just the facts, ma'am..." Sam leaned over and kissed her softly on the cheek — the uninjured one. She turned to face him. "Jessie, I'd love to stay with you tonight, but I'm thinking the ambiance isn't quite what we might have chosen." One of the officers was walking toward their car, probably to check that Jessica was all right.

"What with Sargent Friday stopping by to visit and my aching body, I think you might be right." She rolled down her window. "Give us a moment?" she asked the officer. He waved and walked back to his car. "I think we made a good call on waiting for the right ambiance for our first kiss. We should stick with that plan."

They walked to the door. She had forgotten to turn on the porch light when she left, and was glad of that now. Their kiss was far more brief this time, but it still sent delightful chills down Jessie's spine.

"Good night, Jessie. I'll call before we take off for the mountains tomorrow after work. Have a good weekend. Stay safe. We'll go watch the fireworks next week."

"Mmm...fireworks," she said, a seductive lilt to her voice.

CHAPTER 40

Chase Kovac was growing impatient. He had changed motels every night, using different names each time. Tanner was avoiding him, not answering most of his calls or offering bullshit reasons to delay meeting him with the rest of the money. And he insisted on money — cash. Not some check from DOT Associates, which he figured would bounce. This was a distraction he didn't need. His focus should be on getting the girl to go to the cops and "admit" she was wrong. If those fucking joggers hadn't shown up, he was certain she would have complied with his demands already.

No problem. He had a plan for her.

Tanner was another matter. Kovac figured he couldn't show up at DenDev or at Tanner's home without the cops being all over him. He needed more information.

"Hello. May I speak with Oakley Tanner?" He lowered the pitch of his voice, just in case the company receptionist might recognize it. "I see. When will he be returning to the office?" "No, that's okay. I'll try again next week."

Just as he figured. Tanner wasn't at work, and they weren't giving any information about when he might return. Had he been arrested? Taken off on his own? He needed to find out.

Kovac decided he'd have to take the risk of scoping out Tanner's house. But that would have to wait. He had important preparations to make.

***

"Unbelievable." Jessica scowled at her phone. Paula Miramonte had just called to read her the riot act about the lack of work she was getting done. When Jessica had asked her boss if she was aware that she had been attacked less than two days ago, Miramonte didn't seem to hear a word she said. She simply continued a speech about the pressure being placed on the whole department, and insisted that Jessica meet some deadlines she had never heard of before.

Jessica had managed to hold her tongue, but now questioned why she had bothered.

She decided another session of soaking in the hot tub at the Rec Center was in order. Detective Freeman had vetoed a trip to the mall (Jessie loved sporting goods stores) or a hike in the foothills. Not that she was prohibited from those outings, just that the police thought they were very bad ideas. Maybe just curl up with a book.

Her day was brightened by calls from Sam, who promised to call again as soon as he got back from the weekend's training climb, and from Jamie, who offered to stop by that evening to visit and catch up. He and Greg had a volleyball game after work (of course), but would come over afterwards.

By the time Jessica returned home from her hot tub session, she had decided she felt up to joining her friends the next day for another climbing outing. She called Marilyn to let her know.

***

Jamie was beside himself when he saw her face. "Oh my god, Jessie. What happened?"

She offered up the same abbreviated details of the attack which she had told to Sam.

"You should have called us. Greg and I can stay tonight. You haven't been here alone, have you?"

"Hey, I'm all right. Marilyn and Jordan stayed with me that first night, but now I've got my very own surveillance team hanging around out there, so I'm fine."

That had required a bit more explanation.

"So, what have I missed at work?"

Jamie groaned. "It's a mess. Rumors flying, management acting all flakey and pissy. I'm getting a strong sense that they're getting ready to lay off a bunch of people. They've let on that there's some big scandal involving some sort of hack of our software, and their answer is to hire some big guns in security practices and marketing. And legal — especially legal. I think they're expecting some lawsuits and are trying to pull up the drawbridges. Meanwhile, us peons are probably going to be tossed into the moat."

"You think *you're* going to be canned?"

"Could be. And you too, Jessie. At least, I'd say it's a good idea to be thinking about what we'll do if we get that pink slip."

"Wow." She had gotten through all the medical bills, helped considerably by the money from the special programming assignment. Now she might have to look for a new job. Maybe even pay back the money from what now seemed to be an assignment that was illegal. She wished for the hundredth time that she had never been involved in any of this mess.

"Hey, sorry to be such a party pooper. You've got enough crazy stuff going on without me adding to the pile. Gimme a hug." Jamie believed that everything could be made better with a hug. She complied, happily.

They visited for a little longer, but Jessica hinted that she was getting tired. More hugs all around and the men departed, waving goodnight to Jessica and to the officers in the surveillance car for good measure.

CHAPTER 41

Jessica and friends arrived at North Table Mountain early on Saturday morning, hoping to get on some climbs before it became too crowded and before the day heated up too much. Jessica was glad her sunglasses tended to cover some of her facial bruises, and figured many climbers wouldn't even ask about the scrapes on her arms. Rock rash — scratches and abrasions from rough rock — wasn't all that unusual in this adventurous crowd.

As she had hoped, she was able to lose herself in the climbing, pushing all the stress of recent days out of her conscious mind. She was thrilled that Detective Freeman had given her a green light on getting out with her friends. LaKeisha seemed satisfied with her being out in a group setting, carpooling with friends and returning home with those same friends.

Jessica was fed up with being afraid. She was tired of sitting back while her friends took the lead for all the climbs. She was tired of avoiding rappelling. She was tired of hanging back while they did the work of moving ropes and cleaning gear from the climbing anchors when that involved anything the least bit risky.

She knew how to manage the risks of climbing and rappelling. It was time to climb back up on that horse.

Marilyn reached the top anchor of her second climb of the day, and Jordan lowered her back down. Jessica had taken a short break to munch on an energy bar and drink a little water, and had picked out another climb for the trio to move to.

"I've got this," she said as she headed toward a break in the cliff that offered access to the top via a short scramble. Her plan was to retrieve the slings at the top of the climb they had just finished, pull up the rope, then shift the gear to a different anchor about fifteen feet away. The climb she had selected for them to try next was a challenging one that none of them felt confident of leading. The top rope setup would let them all practice the difficult moves without concerns about falling.

"Jessie, are you sure?" Marilyn called after her. "The anchor is hard to reach — my arms are longer. I can do it."

"I know, but I'm on it. I'll put in some gear so I can lean over and reach it." She scurried around the bend in the trail and headed for the top of the mesa.

Jessica walked along the flat top, occasionally inching her way to the edge so she could get a bearing on where she was. Some routes ended by broad, easy-to-access spots on the undulating edge. The one she was looking for required climbing around and over some boulders, then leaning far over a rock formation that resembled a safety barrier you might see on a curve of a mountain road.

She found the spot she wanted. She leaned slightly over the rock barrier, confirming that their rope and anchor sling were below. The natural rock bench was roughly hip high on Jessica's short frame. She leaned over it again and reached down, judging how much farther she would need to scoot forward to grab the gear. Some climbers — particularly those with much longer arms

— would clean this anchor without tying themselves into something. Jessica knew that was much too risky for her to try.

She stood up and looked around, searching for the right sort of crack in the rocks behind her to use for a safety anchor. Spotting a likely candidate, she placed a camming device from her harness into the crack, and examined her work. It looked good. She attached a long sling to the temporary anchor, tugged on it to test that the hardware was strongly wedged into the crack, and edged her way back to the rock barrier.

She attached the end of the sling to her harness and laid across the rock. She reached straight down the face of the cliff for the climbing anchor. She was just able to touch the fingertips of one hand to one of the two large bolts holding the gear. She tried to scoot forward another few inches, but her safety system wouldn't let her budge. She backed up enough to be able to clasp the shorter sling she always kept cinched to her harness — her personal anchor system or P.A.S. — then tried to use the carabiner at the end of that sling to extend her reach. Not enough.

She began to slide back onto her feet when she heard someone call out, "Hey — need a hand?" She twisted to glance over her shoulder and was surprised to see a climber scrambling over the rocks behind her.

Green helmet, small earring in one ear. "Sam? What are you doing here? I thought you'd be climbing all weekend with your Rainier team." She started to slide further back from the edge, grimacing at the pressure this put on her abdomen, which was still tender from the attack earlier in the week. Sliding back and forth on the rock wasn't helping any.

"Yeah. Well, one guy got sick, so we came back early." He crouched, his back toward her, and examined the camming device she had stuck in the crack. "Let me help you with this.

We'll get this done and then we can visit. Do you need it to be longer?"

Jessica was quite happy to see Sam, but also glad to get some help with the anchor. "Yeah, maybe another foot." She relaxed as best she could while he fiddled with her setup.

"Okay, that should do it."

"You sound a little hoarse. I hope you didn't catch what your friend has." Jessica slid forward on her stomach once more. She felt the tug of the safety sling on her harness as she leaned further out, now with her entire upper body hanging vertically down the cliff face. She looked down at the ground far below, feeling a wave of fear. Marilyn and Jordan had moved beneath the next climb she had picked out and were sitting on their packs, talking and taking a break.

Calm. Calm. Deep breaths. Calm.

She reached for the gear, pulling the rope and carabiners up toward her a bit to make it easier to work. Her P.A.S. dangled below her. She thought it might be helpful for holding the rope's weight while she worked, and started to clip it.

Jessica felt Sam's hands grasp her ankles. She smiled. Okay, so I got a little extra security going on here. It's still a big step toward getting over my fear.

She felt herself slide forward another inch, and gasped, despite herself. His hands were still holding her, but she realized with a shock that there was no tension on her harness from the anchor behind her.

"Fuckin' bitch. This is it. Last chance. You're going to tell the cops *today* that you lied." His harsh voice was barely loud enough for her to hear. Her field of vision shrunk to a small circle encompassing only her arms stretched below her and the anchor. She could barely breath.

"Back off *today*. Say it — say it!" His voice was filled with fury. He lifted her legs above the rock bench, the edge cutting across her upper thighs as she slid further down the cliff face.

Jessica screamed in terror, despite knowing that no one could possibly climb up to her in time to help. He let go of her ankles with an abrupt shove as he turned to sprint away across the flat-topped mesa.

Time slowed. Jessica felt herself falling headfirst, then beginning to flip. A blur of rock rushed past, then a glimpse of blue sky as her body folded and rotated. Her upper arm and hip slammed hard against rock just as she felt a sharp pain at her waist.

Her ears were filled with screams and shouts. She was dazed, momentarily confused. The sounds were coming from below her. No, some were from above as well. She began to process what had happened. Her P.A.S. was stretched above her, clipped to one of the large anchor bolts, holding her in place a body-length from the top of the cliff.

She began to piece thoughts and memories together. She didn't know if it had been some subconscious instinct or simply fear, but she owed her life to a last instant decision to clip herself to the bolt instead of the loose rope.

"Jessie, are you all right? Are you hurt?" A man was standing at the cliff's edge off to her right. She focused on him, trying to figure out who he might be.

"Jessie?" He tugged on his earlobe. "I'm Jordan. Talk to me!"

"I'm just a little banged up, I think. I'm okay. I'm okay." She muttered it again and again, trying to convince herself. She looked around, spotting other climbers scurrying around on top of the cliff with gear and ropes. Below her, Marilyn was hurriedly tying in to the rope that dangled beside her, the loose one she had *not* clipped into.

"We're going to set up a bomber anchor up here and I'll lower down to you. We'll rig up a system to get you down," Jordan said, as he worked his way around the boulders at the top of the cliff, maneuvering closer to her position.

"No. You don't need to do that. I can rappel from here. I'm okay." Jessica grasped both sides of the dangling rope and pinched them to form a bight on each piece. She fed the bights through her belay device and secured the system to a large carabiner attached to the front of her harness.

She looked down at Marilyn, who had let the rope loose. She looked intently at the coils of rope on the ground, confirming that both ends were safely resting there.

"Is the rope down?" she asked.

"Yes. Both ends. It's safe to rappel," Marilyn confirmed, her hands wrapped around both sides of the dangling rope.

Jessica used the system to cinch herself a bit higher so she could unclip the P.A.S. sling from the anchor.

"On rappel," she announced, and lowered herself safely to Marilyn's side. They grabbed each other desperately. Jessica's legs couldn't hold her. They sank to the ground together, holding each other tight and rocking.

"What happened?" Marilyn finally asked. "Did your gear come out?"

Before she could answer, they heard shouts from above. "We've got him pinned. The police are on their way."

Marilyn's mouth dropped open. Jessica sprawled out flat on her back. She stared at the cliff. "I thought he was Sam."

Marilyn sat beside her, and held her hand.

"I didn't back off. I'm done with backing off."

CHAPTER 42

It was early evening before Jordan pulled up in Jessica's driveway. During the ride home, Marilyn had ordered a pizza delivery, since they all were starving. The police had offered snacks from their vending machines to tide them over during the long hours of interviews, but the food wasn't the least bit appealing.

Detective Freeman spent much of her time talking to Jessica. Other officials came and went throughout the afternoon, but she had difficulty keeping track of names, and the parade of faces left her thoroughly confused. She was surprised to be introduced to an FBI Agent at one point, and to learn that the Feds had been consulting on the case for some time.

Jordan and Marilyn were also interviewed extensively, as were two climbers who had spotted Kovac trying to run away just after Jessica screamed. They had climbed up top to clean an anchor, just as Jessica was trying to do, and were able to run down the man as he tried to flee. They tackled him and pinned him to the ground, soon to be reinforced by others who scrambled to the top of the mesa.

Jordan grabbed some plates and silverware from the kitchen and set them out on the table while Jessica went to lay down for a few minutes. Her body ached all over. The main impact with the cliff wall had been to her hip, and she suspected that her neck had snapped back when she hit — it was extremely stiff. She had insisted that she didn't need to see a doctor, and had downed generous doses of ibuprofen to get by.

Marilyn shook her gently. She had dozed off. "You have a call. Detective Freeman." She handed Jessica her phone which had been sitting in the kitchen.

"I have some good news, Jessica. We've just picked up Donald Oakley Tanner. He was getting ready to board a flight to Jamaica. The Feds are saying they're ready to charge both Tanner and Kovac with a laundry list of charges related to the money scam that spanned multiple states. And I just got off the phone with the DA's office. They've got another list of charges to cover everything the Feds can't touch.

"We've tied Tanner to the DOT Associates checking account they used to pay you for programming, and we've tracked down most of the other bank accounts he used. Kovac had a rental receipt in his car for the green helmet he was wearing when we arrested him, plus printed instructions on caring for a newly-pierced ear. There's more, but just be assured that we have strong evidence against both of them."

"That's such a relief. Thank you, LaKeisha. You and Detective Fugate have been so helpful. I can't believe it's finally over."

"Jessica, I've got to warn you that it's not like they'll be toted off to prison tomorrow and you can forget all about them. You should expect to be asked to testify, and a case like this could drag on for years. But I'm optimistic about getting these two locked up for quite some time. They're both tripping over themselves pointing the finger at the other guy. I think we've got a strong case, and I'm confident it'll get even stronger when the DNA results come in."

"I understand."

"Best of luck, Jessica. You're a brave lady."

She set the phone down and sat quietly for a few minutes. The doorbell rang and she heard someone go to the door. "Pizza's here, Jess," Marilyn shouted.

She didn't have to be told twice.

***

Sam called the next night, back home from a weekend of climbing snow-filled gullies, camping on the snow, and practicing crevasse rescue techniques.

"Hi, Jessie. How was your weekend? Are you feeling better?"

She had been debating with herself all day about what to tell him over the phone. "Hi, Sam. I had some really..." She still was unsure what words to use. "... *significant* things happen while you were gone."

"Oh?" He sounded worried, unsure where she was going with this.

"Sam, it would mean a lot to me if you could come over. Tonight."

He paused, trying to interpret what she was really saying.

"I know you must be tired from being out climbing all weekend, but I really want to see you. I know we haven't known each other all that long, but you've become very important to me, and I...I really want to see you. In person," she added.

He smiled. "I can do 'in person.' Let me jump in the shower and change into normal clothes, and I can be there in a half hour."

She sighed in relief. "Thanks, Sam. See you soon."

***

He pulled the cushioned chair close to the couch, and they sat face to face, both leaning forward, hands clasped as she told her story. For the first time since this spiral of confusion and threats, fear and pain had begun, Jessica let herself cry. Sam moved beside her on the couch, holding her in his arms, her face buried in his chest.

Finally she ran out of tears. It was very late, and both were exhausted physically and emotionally. They went to the bedroom where they pulled off their shoes. Jessica undressed down to her underwear, and Sam gasped at her bruises — some from the attack during her walk, some from yesterday's fall. She crawled under the covers as he stripped to his underwear. He climbed into bed and took her in his arms, gently kissing her forehead as she snuggled close.

"We need a signal. Some way for you to know it's really me," Sam whispered.

"Jordan pulls on his ear," she said.

"Ah. I've seen him do that. I wondered what that was about." He thought a moment. "How about this?" He held up his free hand, forming a "V" between the second and third fingers. "Live long and prosper."

"I'll know it's either you or Spock. Or Rabbi Zwerkin," she said.

"Oh. Do you think you might confuse me with the Rabbi?"

"Not likely. He retired years ago. He's about eighty-five and has white hair. Just don't cover your ears so I can tell if you have pointed ears or not." She yawned.

"Sleep tight, Jessie. No more bad guys."

223

"Not as long as I'm here with my good guy," she whispered. "Good night."

They were both asleep within minutes.

CHAPTER 43

"I have a business proposition for you." Jamie was grinning broadly as he moved his empty plate aside and pulled a folder out of his briefcase.

"I don't know if I ever want to hear another business proposition," Jessica said. Still, she looked curiously at the folder he had placed on the table in front of him. Their waitress swept by, clearing their empty dishes.

"This one is legal."

"That's a good start."

"Jessie, I've decided to go out on my own. I'm tired of working for someone else. I don't like the politics, having layers of people to go through in order to find out what the client needs, the red tape."

Jessica was nodding as he ticked off his list. Been there, hated that.

"So, what I'd like to propose is that we become partners. Form our own consulting business. We've both got contacts and I've already got a company interested in using us to develop a custom system."

She started to speak, but he plunged forward. "We'd both have to do a bit of everything. Get back to our roots of heads-down programming as well as all our design and implementation work. We'll have to deal with billing and documentation and —"

"— and testing and training and marketing." She smiled. "We need to really sit down and go over the business plan, but...it sounds wonderful!"

He jumped to his feet and rushed around the table, pulling her to her feet and giving her a hug. "I know we can make this work, Jessie. Wait, wait. I've started working on a business plan." He returned to his side of the table and waved the folder triumphantly.

"I'm not surprised," she said with a laugh. "Okay, let's dig in and see how this can work."

***

Jamie had read the writing on the wall accurately. When Jessica returned home from their lunch, she received a call from the big boss himself, Richard De Graaf.

"Jessie, you've been with us for a long time, and that's why I wanted to personally call you to tell you what's going on. I won't sugar-coat it. DenDev is facing some serious challenges. A group of clients is threatening legal action based on their contention that we failed to provide sufficient security in our software to prevent this incident from happening. Despite the fact that we are paying back all the lost funds to our clients immediately so they won't have to wait for the legal process to play out, we are under pressure to make some significant, immediate changes."

Where is this leading? she wondered.

"We are hiring a security consultant firm to help us out. We're going to want to build a team of our own people to take their recommendations and implement them. Jessie, I'd like you to be on that team. The consultants will be designing the system and providing programming specifications, so we'll need a couple of top-notch programmers to get the coding done. Can I count on you to be one of them?"

Jessica grimaced. Perhaps she had misunderstood. "So, would I be doing any design work? You know that's really my forte."

"I realize that, and you are quite good at it. However, all the security design work would be handled by the consultant team. This is where you are needed, Jessie. We're putting all the new design projects on hold for the time being. Our focus needs to be on security and continuing to provide support for our existing software. We'll be cutting back considerably on our development staff, I'm afraid, so you should consider yourself fortunate. Sadly, we are having to lay off most of the people in your department."

"I see." She thought about spending her days programming again, simply working from specs written by someone else. It sounded like a huge step backward, like the sort of work she had done her first year out of grad school. She thought of the risks but exciting challenges of starting a small consulting firm with Jamie. And she knew what she needed to do.

"Richard, thank you for offering me this position, but I'm going to decline. In fact, I'm giving you two weeks notice that I will be leaving DenDev. Do you need an email or a printed letter from me to that effect?"

There was silence on the line. "Jessie, are you sure of this?"

"Absolutely."

"Well, I'm sorry to hear that. We've been offering a compensation package to the others who we've had to let go, and

I'll make sure you receive that same package. I'll have someone send that over to you via email by the end of the day. Take care, Jessie."

"You, too. Goodbye."

Jessica sat quietly, reflecting on all the changes that had come to her life in the past several weeks and months. This latest leap in faith seemed huge, but it felt right.

I'm not going to back off. She let out a yelp of victory (sending Pooka diving under the couch) and placed a call to Jamie to tell him she was *in*.

CHAPTER 44

"Come with me to Washington. You can play tourist while I'm climbing Rainier, and then we can go play. We'll hang with my brother near Seattle for a couple of days, but then we'll be on our own. I'll bet I can extend my vacation several extra days. I've got a bunch of personal days built up." Sam was beaming his intoxicating smile. "You said you and Jamie won't be starting work with your first client for another couple of weeks. Come on, Jessie. It'll be great."

Jessica's mind was racing. She was used to planning things out well in advance, figuring out each little detail. But her life was accelerating forward at a pace she had never dreamed of.

Forget all that. This sounds wonderful.

"Okay. Let's do it," she laughed, giddy with excitement.

"Yes!" Sam pumped his fist. "We should celebrate!"

Just then, the first rockets shot high into the air, bursting into enormous spheres of red, white, and blue. Bang - bang - bang! The crowd around them cheered as the fireworks display continued, accompanied by a Sousa march.

"Look, everyone's celebrating!" he shouted over the cacophony.

They held hands as they watched the Independence Day show. The finale was completed and the noise level began to ease.

"We should celebrate," Jessica said, her lips close to Sam's ear.

"What would you like to do?"

"Mmm...fireworks," she whispered, nibbling on his ear.

"Perfect. We can stop on the way home to pick up some tiramisu."

ABOUT THE AUTHOR

Diane Winger is a self-described "retired software geek" who loves hiking, rock climbing, and cross-country skiing when she isn't glued in front of her computer playing around with website designs, watching cat videos, and writing. If you meet her for only the third or fourth time, don't be surprised if she doesn't recognize you.

She and her husband, Charlie, are co-authors of several guidebooks on outdoor recreation. They now live in western Colorado, but Diane spent most of her life in Denver. This is her first novel.

WingerBookstore.com

***

If you enjoyed **Faces**, please consider writing a review on Amazon.com.

Made in the USA
Las Vegas, NV
01 September 2024

94643728R00134